Six Mile Store

Deixis Press
Copyright © A. M. Belsey 2026
All rights reserved.

The right to be identified as the author of this work has been asserted by A. M. Belsey in accordance with the Copyright, Designs and Patents Act 1988.

This book is a work of fiction. Names, characters, businesses, and incidents either are products of the author's imagination or are used in a fictitious manner. Any resemblance to actual persons, living or dead, events, or locales is entirely coincidental.

Quotation from *Fear and Loathing in Las Vegas*, 1971, used with permission from The Gonzo Trust

First published in 2026 by Deixis Press
www.deixis.press

ISBN 978-1-917090-12-4

Cover design by Deividas Jablonskis

Typeset using Sabon LT Pro

Six Mile Store

A. M. BELSEY

DEIXIS PRESS

For Kim, who is in here a lot.

"This is not a good town for psychedelic drugs. Reality itself is too twisted."

—HUNTER S. THOMPSON

THE BEGINNING

The store had always been there. By the time it got into your blood, it was already old, grimy and hunkered down by the side of the road in a way that seemed like it was growing out of the foothills it neighbored. It sat on a crossroads, linking nowhere to nowhere.

In those days, travellers moving swiftly from west to east found this squatting, dirty gnome with its lonely gas pumps at exactly the right spot, just far enough out of town to make them feel relieved that, no, they didn't miss their last chance to fuel up before heading into another long stretch of nothing. There, too, were the travellers confused by similar numbers. A 64 is a little like a 65, perhaps, unless you are on the kind of roads where one stretch of nowhere gets you to Minnesota and the other gets you to North Carolina.

When you were very small you had no desire to go to Minnesota or North Carolina or anywhere else. You just wanted to go to the store and pad around in the sawdust on the floor, staring at the wonders on display: a huge box filled with nothing but corn kernels, shivery and cold on your fingers and strangely solid when you plunge your hand in. A cooler full of live worms wriggling happily before their own final, fatal, shivery plunge. Unfathomably giant sacks of animal feed. Dusty candy wrappers on bottom shelves—candy cigarettes, Sixlets, MoonPies. The hulking man sitting silently behind the counter, hawkishly watching the fuel pumps. That man's missing hand.

You lived only a quarter of a mile away from the store, but you could never, ever walk there. The highway was death for any creature: a skunk, your own dogs, a girl from your class who walked along the side one New Year's Eve. You always had to be driven, and you often begged to go. Where else could you see a teenage girl hauling two 50-pound sacks of animal feed, one over each shoulder? Have you ever seen a 4'11" woman poking a 30-yard stick into a hole to measure how much fuel remains far beneath the ground, while her fat silent husband gazes impassively past her? How about a huge, gleaming meat slicer, open to the largest setting, daring you to put your fingers near it?

HONEY

Saturday, 18 July

As I hop on the spot, breath clouding the dark air, Sam Legs opens up the store, the aluminum sliding door screeching upward. The store itself seems to breathe deeply, to wake up and stretch as we walk in. Sam Legs wears her usual morning cheerfulness; I feel as foggy as the air outside. Lights on, pumps on, coffee on, registers unlocked.

The door tinkles open. One of our morning regulars comes in for his Mountain Dew and Skoal, drops a quarter into the kidney transplant box, then leaves without saying much of anything. Most of our usual early customers are more like me than Sam Legs, thank god.

I look out the window at the pink and orange sunrise and try to open my eyes, to figure out what the hell happened the previous night. I conclude that we just drank too much and talked too loud and slept not enough, but nothing about any of that justifies the dread I am feeling now. I look in my handbag for money to buy my own coffee, and I find that I have inadvertently brought a roach clip into work. It is inside my sock—the one I couldn't find, but then grabbed off the living room floor and shoved in the bag at the very last minute before easing Lynn's screen door shut.

"Hello?" I look up and a woman—Shirley, another regular—is glaring at me. I think she has just asked me for cigarettes. I have to card her, as always, though anyone who looked for more than a second at this woman would see weariness and age. She pays me with a handful of coins. If I could put a tracker on this change, I know I'd learn it's the same money I handed to Shirley's skinny, dirty kids the night before when they each came in, one by one, to hand me a $1 food stamp and a piece of Dubble Bubble. I look impassively at Shirley's desperate face and tell her to have a nice day.

Last night I was drifting again. I finished college last month, and summer's damp aimlessness has got into my bones. Often I find myself avoiding the return to my tiny, dark apartment: cruising the strip, gazing into the eyes of strangers. Arkansas late at night is syrupy hot, and all the good Christians are tucked up sober in their beds by 9pm. At 11 or 1 or 3 it is just us aimless pot smokers, driving

Six Mile Store

at 15mph and peering dimly at the Taco Bell, which always seems to recede even as it is getting closer. We inhabit the Waffle House, the Wal-Mart, the Denny's, strangers' living rooms, strangers' bedrooms, strangers' bathroom floors.

I straggle around town, going from home to friends' houses to work. Last night I found myself parking up in front of Lynn's house, hand in my purse to buy some pot, and some of his attention along with it.

His apartment is one of the octagons over on Elm Street, funny mushroom-shaped double-deckers painted in a drab khaki, all clustered together like a Smurf village. Inside he's made it cozy, the prettiest drug den you've ever seen, with framed New Yorker covers on the walls and blankets his grandmother crocheted for him on his couch and bed.

"I went to see that Vowan guy last week," I said, settling in with a beer in front of his television, watching Madonna gyrate through the Ray of Light video, thrusting her weird bellybutton at us. "Did I tell you I won't have to pay them anything? They're going to pay *me* if I teach a couple of freshman classes and do a little private tutoring. I even get a free dorm room."

"Why are you doing a Masters at that Baptist college though?" he sniffed. "Aren't you worried you'll burst into flames when someone prays?" Lynn knows I don't have a lot of use for church; I went to church—a lot of churches, actually—for a long time, but one of them threw me out for going to another one. Suffice it to say, some churches think they've got God on the other end of their telephone, and hell knows it ain't a party line.

"They didn't ask me if I've been excommunicated. I didn't volunteer to tell them. I'll be sure to wear flame retardant underwear."

Lynn snorted. "Underwear. That'll be a novelty for you. Wanna smoke?" he asked. I was surprised; usually he tried not to dip into his own stash too much—but, then again, I guess I had just bought it, so it was mine now.

"Where's your roomie?" I asked. I could never remember that guy's name.

"No idea," Lynn said, and out came the tequila.

I vaguely remember, now, that later on, after way too many shots, Lynn and I were arguing about my love life. I've never understood what his problem is with me seeing Karim. I'm pretty sure Lynn's got a girlfriend somewhere too, not that our other relationships matter that much to either of us when the two of us get drunk or high or lonely, like last night.

"You ok?" Sam Legs is looking at me with concern. Surprisingly, I find that I am fine, since I got the coffee in me, and I say so. In fact, I feel almost cheerful—not as cheerful as Sam Legs, though, not that I ever am. I wonder how someone with a cage on her leg can be so chipper. Her left leg is shorter than her right one. She says the doctor broke it and now she has to keep it broken by turning the screws on the cage every so often. Keeping it broken is the only way it can grow.

Billy Wayne comes over about 7 as usual. He is wearing my favorite of his outfits: the red shorts/yellow hard hat/cowboy boot combo. No shirt this time.

Six Mile Store

This morning: a six-pack of toilet paper. When I work with Michelle, she always asks, watching Billy Wayne cross the highway, "How does one man use that much toilet paper?" I also wonder what Billy Wayne does with the toilet paper, but I have my own theory about the toothpicks. I think he's building something with them, maybe a life-size model of a lawnmower, since he does love his lawnmowers so much. I haven't yet figured out how he's sticking them together, though.

"Is that all for you, Billy Wayne?"

He sort of grunts at me and stares out the window. "Gonna be a hot day," he eventually says. He wants a bag for his toilet paper; I don't even need to ask. Michelle gets annoyed when Billy Wayne asks for bags, since he only ever buys one thing at a time, but I wouldn't want to carry a naked pack of toilet paper across a highway either.

He gives me the money and I cash him out. As always, he counts his change intently before he heads out the door, holding it tight in his hand. No pockets in this morning's outfit, but I am sure he will be over in his denim cutoffs later.

Even though Billy Wayne comes in several times a day, he is a mystery. He lives with his elderly mother, but nobody ever sees her. He has a car, but I don't think he can drive. He hoards toilet paper and toothpicks, and he has three riding lawnmowers, which he rides around his lawn, but with the blades off. "Why you got three lawnmowers, Billy Wayne?" Sam Legs asked him once. "You can't ride more than one at a time." This question seemed to flummox him. He just likes lawnmowers.

Michelle gossiped a couple weeks ago that Billy Wayne got in trouble with his momma a while back for trying to get a hooker to come visit. I can't imagine that; he's so childlike that I can't imagine his appetites have developed past around age 10. But I can't be sure of anything when it comes to Billy Wayne.

At 7am I was feeling fine; at 10am I understand that's because I've been drunk the whole time.

Around 10:15am I excuse myself to the restroom. I sit astraddle the toilet and lean my hot, dry face against the cistern. I can't cry—crying would make my head pound even harder. I feel beyond sick—no chance of food, but no chance of surviving without food.

I reflect on how Rhonda made me clean this restroom with a toothbrush—a literal toothbrush—about three months ago, before Roger made her take a break from work. I wonder if anyone else has been forced to do that kind of project more recently. I could use a lie-down on the floor.

I splash cold water on my tight, screaming skin, then rummage in my bag for some painkillers. I don't have any, but I do find a little note from Karim on that blue scented paper he uses, written in his oddly flowery handwriting: "My heart is yours, *aşkım*." It makes me feel a little better, enough to go out and face my customers.

It's a quiet time, 10:45 on a Saturday morning. When I come out, that faith healer is back. She's the one who saw Michelle's bandaged thumb last week and asked her what happened. When Michelle told her, the woman offered to heal her. Michelle let her try—it's cheaper than the doctor, I guess.

I didn't scream when Michelle cut her thumb off in May. Nobody did. We heard the slicer make a curiously satisfying sound, and we saw her blood dripping thickly on the cheese. We saw Michelle's face the color of deli paper. I silently picked up the thumb, much smaller than I thought a thumb would be, and I wrapped it in a paper towel. Then I realized I was yelling at Sam Legs, and that she was running toward me with a cup of ice.

"Turn that slicer to the thickest you can get it," the woman in her Sunday finest had demanded. It's a common request, for bacon or cheese or bologna. Michelle did as she was told.

You can trust church women, you know. You can trust them to behave like entitled, self-righteous brats, I mean. All these ladies bark orders in their best dresses, radiating their disdain for godless teenagers working on a Sunday. They would be equally incensed if the store were closed on Sunday, of course, because they need their quarter-pound of ham and their thick-sliced cheddar. And you can trust them to ask—while you're on the phone to 911 as your colleague slumps to the floor in shock—"What about my cheese?"

Screw the church ladies. Give me bikers any day. If Sunday lunchtime is the worst time to be working, Sunday early morning is the best. Those men in their leather clothes and giant beards roll up on their noisy motorcycles. They stroll in like they own you and everything around them. Then they come to the counter and it's all "Please, ma'am, may I have a sandwich when you get some time?" "Miss, if you've got a second would you please get me a pack of Marlboro Reds?" "Thank you, ma'am, you have a good day." And off they roar.

"20 Virginia Slims, and 10 on gas," the faith healer says. I think about asking her if she can cure my hangover, but I don't want Sam Legs to hear. But as I'm handing her her change, she grips my hand and looks at me with raw intensity. "You need to look for a sign," she says, squeezing my fingers.

"Oh, I will," I say brightly, flashing her a neon grin. With these weirdos, we've all learned the best thing you can do is agree with them until they leave.

Billy Wayne comes in again, wearing his denim shorts. He buys his toothpicks. This time, though, I test a theory I've been turning over in my head for some time. I short his change by a full quarter. He intently counts it, then he wiggles it into his little denim pocket and walks out.

At 2:25pm, just before the end of my shift, someone pulls up in a beat-up tan and white Volvo—right in front of the door, like nobody ever does. The driver gets out. It's some flat-faced middle-aged woman I've never seen before.

"Hey," she announces as the door tinkles. "I just came in to see Rhonda. Is she around?"

Now, Rhonda lives right across the road, but I'm not going to tell a stranger that. I say, "Rhonda isn't here right now. Can I let her know you came?"

"Oh sure," she says. "I'm Lisa. She's in my aerobics class and I haven't seen her in so long. I remember she said she owns this place." She leans right over the counter and grabs my newspaper and a pen from behind the register. "Could you give her my number? I'd love to catch up with her," she says as she writes.

After Lisa drives off, I clock out, say goodbye to Sam Legs, and walk over to Rhonda's house. When she answers the door, I'm a little shocked. Rhonda is looking bad. I haven't seen her in a good couple of weeks—she does come in the store, but only sometimes—and I notice that she has got thinner and puffier all at once, somehow. I heard she had been shooting at some people's dogs for getting in her yard. But there are some things we tolerate about each other in small towns, like that guy who walks around T. J. Maxx asking to suck women's toes, or that boy who keeps getting caught breaking into that church of Christ up in Enola and fiddling with himself in the pews. Rhonda's sick with something, we say. So what if she shot your dog?

I tell her about her visitor. "Oh, Lisa," she says. "Bless her heart for thinking of me. How did she look?"

Like John Denver, I think, but instead I say, "Well, she seemed energetic."

Something comes over Rhonda's face, a red paleness, and I realize Rhonda is angry. At me? Lisa? Herself? I've seen this before, so I don't wait to find out. I don't want to end up scrubbing Rhonda's personal toilet with a toothbrush. "Anyway, she gave me her phone number. I didn't tell her you lived here."

Rhonda looks past me. "Honey, could you take the charity box up to the bank for me? I don't feel so good right now. Just tell them you want to put it in the Six Mile Amy account."

I really want to go home, have a shower, get the onions off my hands. But Rhonda isn't in any state to leave the house. So I go back into the store to get the box, then into my car and up to town, past the catfish house and the Assembly of God. As I pass the newest strip mall in town, I notice one of the Jennifers from my high school graduating class opening up one of the units. She is wearing a leotard and some legwarmers.

Linda, one of the tellers, smiles as I walk up. "Good to see you, honey. What you got today?"

"Just the charity box for Amy," I say. "Rhonda asked me to deposit it. How's she doing?" Linda is related to Amy somehow, one of these third cousins or second aunts or something we always keep vague track of around here.

"Oh, she's in a bad way. She has to be at the dialysis clinic seems like every day, all day. Her daddy's working hard as he can, but he just can't keep up the bills. It's so good of y'all to keep this box out for her. Tell Rhonda hi for me."

Amy's box is not by any means the first box we have put out for sick people. We've got plenty of health problems in this area: bad hearts, bad kidneys, premature babies, workplace accidents, rodeo accidents. There was that kid, too, who accidentally shot himself in the chin while hunting—though that money was more for his funeral, I guess. For a while there was a new charity box every week, but Amy's has been there for a long time now. I wonder briefly, meanly, if Amy's unending kidney transplant campaign is dooming some other local kid to die from, say, childhood leukemia.

On my way home, passing by that strip mall again, I catch a glimpse of that white and tan Volvo, the same one

Six Mile Store

from before, sitting outside Jennifer's unit. I slow down to drive past and see that Lisa woman ushering a miniature version of herself into the building. The kid is frowning, then gone from view.

Sunday, 19 July

Last night I briefly considered calling my parents for the first time in weeks, but I decided I wasn't in the mood to listen to my father's silence, or my mother's complaints. Instead, I called Karim and invited him over. While I waited for him, I tried to cheer my dismal apartment up a little, lighting some candles and incense, putting in a Sheryl Crow CD, thinking how glad I will be to move out of this place in September.

When Karim came in I didn't even have time to offer him a beer. He began kissing my neck, whispering *"aşkım, aşkım"* while unbuttoning my shirt, moving his hands over my breasts and back. I could smell cigarette smoke in his hair. His lips when they met mine were bitter, but his tongue was sweet and persistent.

As we moved toward my couch I pushed his soft t-shirt upward and caressed the soft hair on his chest and stomach. None of my college boyfriends had Karim's masculinity; they were all pale and hairless like me, and I thought that was my preference until I learned the difference. Seeing his dark, lean torso for the first time had been almost a religious experience, and ever since then I had worshiped him with my body. I sat astride him and, with Sheryl crooning about how love is a good thing, we found a rhythm that suited us both, his mouth on my collarbone and breasts, one hand around my back, the other stroking me in ways no other boyfriend had ever had the imagination, or perhaps patience, to try.

In the morning I found myself waking just as the sky outside began to lighten. Karim's feet were intertwined with mine under my soft flannel sheets. He was curled toward me, his face innocent and boyish in sleep. I touched his cheek, careful not to wake him, knowing soon he would be gone, wondering how I would stand to lose him.

I drive up to the Six Mile Store this afternoon with a renewed sense of enthusiasm for shelf-stacking, having shoved the nagging feeling that I should come up with a comprehensive life plan right to the back of my head, but, as I arrive, I am surprised to see the Volvo from yesterday parked in my usual spot.

Inside, Lisa is not only here, but is in fact behind the counter with Sam Legs, who took the morning shift today. "Hey," Sam Legs says, looking at me with an inscrutable, tight smile. "This is Lisa, our newest employee. She's been training since 9. Are you OK to take over when I go, show her how to stick the pumps before she goes at 3?"

"Sure!" I say, hoping Lisa can't see my confusion. We haven't been looking for a new person, and we don't really need anyone as far as I know, especially now that Michelle is back almost full-time.

"Lisa," Sam Legs says, coming to stand next to me, "we are going to go look at the shifts for next week. Holler if you need help." We walk briskly to the back, leaving Lisa looking a little forlorn at the register, her blunt bob and thin lips drawing straight, neutral lines across her plain face.

Sam Legs is seething. "Rhonda hired her! Apparently she wants an adult running this place. Aren't we adults? Haven't we been running it?" I don't care about running the store myself, but I know Sam Legs has been angling for a manager position, especially with the rumors that Rhonda might be trying to make the store part of a franchise.

"I think they were in some aerobics class together before Rhonda got sick," I say. "I guess she trusts her to do a good job. Come on, don't worry about it."

"Girls!" Lisa sounds vaguely panicked. We poke our heads around the end of the aisle and see two people in line. I wink at Sam Legs. "Aww, shit. If she can't handle that, you've got nothing to worry about."

Karim notwithstanding, this area is white as anything. We did have a little black girl in my class when I was about 6 or 7, but she was gone by the time I was 7 or 8—possibly due to the fact that the Ku Klux Klan joined the Adopt-A-Mile program right next to the school. My companions, my teachers, my friends, have always been white, and the Six Mile customers are no different. Truly hard work, though, brings immigrants, and when road work came near the store, we got a new daily influx of Mexican itinerant workers.

Here's the thing about Spanish down here: it's the only language on offer, and there are only two years of it available.

Six Mile Store

"Get it over with as quick as you can," says our principal, so most people stumble through two years of high school Spanish in 9th and 10th grade, and only then because it's a state requirement if you want your high school diploma.

The Six Mile Store sells sandwiches and hot lunches, but when they encounter people who can't speak English, many of the people I work with just hand them a plate of any old thing. I like trying a little harder, though—figuring out what each guy actually wants. Overalls doesn't want *lechuga*. Hi-viz vest wants *jamón y pollo* all in one sandwich. That kind of thing.

The first thing I learn about Lisa today is that she is an any-old-thing advocate. "Why do you bother?" she asks, with real surprise on her bland face, as I add extra *cebolla* to a hot dog.

There were a bunch of Eastern Europeans at my old college for reasons nobody ever fully explained, specifically a group of Bulgarian musicians. I still hang out with them sometimes, along with their endless rotation of clever-looking little girlfriends, all of them wearing flannel shirts and round glasses. I like musicians despite not being much of one myself; going over there and listening to them jam on their cellos and violas and pianos makes me feel like I am part of something, though I am really on the outskirts.

A couple of months ago, right after that thing with The Cop, I met Karim at one of the house parties. I remember one night the lights were down, we were all high, someone was doing an exceptionally long and beautiful fiddle jam, and I saw Karim—I had seen him before, but I mean I *saw* him, for the first time. He was always in his bathrobe and socks. It turned out that made sense: he lived there.

"You're not a musician," he said, looking over at me. "Why don't you play something?" I felt accused.

"I mean, it's not that I don't want to play, I just don't know how."

"Me neither. How I got in with these guys I don't know." He offered me a cigarette. I'm not really a tobacco smoker, but something about his eyes in that moment made me want to give it a shot. He laughed at my coughing, then handed me a whiskey.

He was from Turkey, there for a year only, he said, heading home at the end of the summer, though he was trying to arrange an extension. By "there" I presumed he meant my college, like the Bulgarians, who were all doing music degrees. I asked him what he studied, and he laughed. "Economics," he said, and looked at me, dark eyes crinkling at the sides even though his mouth wasn't smiling. I didn't have the vaguest idea what Economics could do for a person.

"Sounds good. I'm doing English."

"But you speak English."

"You know, literature. I read books and then talk about them like I'm smart."

"You seem smart to me," he said, then put his hand on the back of my neck and drew me in for a surprisingly aggressive kiss.

We didn't talk really about anything after that. Over time I learned that he was Muslim—not too serious about it, I guess. His family didn't particularly miss him—something we shared—and he didn't miss them. He liked it in Arkansas, the flat wastelands, the fat white women, the winter ice storms and the blazing humidity in summer. He liked all of it, and when I drove around I began to see it through the eyes of a foreigner: all trashed out road signs, sprawl from the semi-urban Conway area littering itself all the way out to Vilonia, a concrete sign telling me to PREPARE TO MEET GOD and JESUS IS COMING SOON.

Speaking of that sign, it has a carving on the side telling us we should have erected it in Algeria in 1990. Nobody did that. There's a twin sign down in Benton that says they should have erected it *on the planet Venus* in 1990, which, by the way, happened to be the year they sent that Magellan probe to Venus. Nobody bothered to smuggle the sign in with the probe, though. I wonder what would have happened if we had followed all the signs' instructions. Then again, maybe we dodged a bullet. The relevant conditions were not met for Jesus's return.

The relevant conditions were met, though, for me to return to Karim's bed, again and again. On many of my off days we lay sprawled in a post-sex coma, smoking pot and halfway watching television. One night, as we got ready for a party the boys were hosting, he gave me a present: a spicy, heavy, sexy perfume that smelled like nothing else I've ever worn, a vaguely bandagey smell underneath spices, like the spices were acting to cover up something rotten or dead. I loved it. Another time, he hand-fed me raw meat, apparently a delicacy in Turkey. I loved it too. I began to wonder if I loved Karim.

Lynn was not pleased when I told him that I'd been seeing Karim. Arguing with Lynn was new and strange. I wondered if his feelings for me had changed, even though we'd always agreed to keep things casual. We have been friends since we were four years old—and friends with benefits for a couple of years. And now I can't think what I was like as a child, or what Lynn was like, or how either of us ended up where we are.

I tell Lisa a little about Karim, in our downtime after the lunch rush, before she heads home. I understand why Sam Legs doesn't want her here, but I think it's going to be kind of nice having someone around to talk to. Rhonda used to be a kind woman, but her illness is too far gone for her to be any kind of maternal figure—which I guess makes sense, given what happened. Lisa tells me a little about her daughter: Lottie, short for Charlotte. It sounds like she adores her and wants her to be able to do all the things that some little girls get obsessed with: dancing, horses, twirling.

Not like my mom. I think back to when I was Lottie's age. Every morning before school I used to pour out my cereal and milk, get myself dressed, go out the screen door and stand at the end of our driveway in the dark, waiting for the bus to come down my way from Saltillo. I knew better than to miss that bus; Mom wasn't the kind of morning person who was ever eager to drive me to school.

The handful of times I did miss the bus, I was always a little afraid to walk in my parents' room: dark and cavernous, sometimes frozen and rattling with the air conditioner in the window, my mother peering out at me from sleep like she didn't know who I was. In the car, she'd drive squinting at the road; silent with her bathrobe on, pumping the pedals with her slippers, hunched forward over the wheel.

Six Mile Store

The afternoons were easier: I came in on the bus and made myself a little dinner—noodles, or a sandwich, or something microwaved from the fridge. Then I turned on the TV and watched Star Trek: The Next Generation, Jeopardy, and Wheel of Fortune while half-assing my homework. That routine had been how my afternoons were spent ever since I was able to come home alone, which my parents made me do from about fourth grade onward. It's no wonder that I'm able to spend time with myself happily, but it also means I never got to do dance lessons or school plays or anything like that. And then once I was old enough to drive, I was too old to start learning that stuff anyway. I envied little Charlotte.

Anyway, Lisa is interested to hear about Karim, and even says her best friend has a Turkish boyfriend too, named Demir. It's crazy to think there are enough Turkish people in the area for there to be two in Lisa's extended circle. I tell her I'll ask Karim if he knows him; maybe it would be good for them to meet. If they miss home maybe they can talk about it with each other.

After Lisa goes home, I'm left with only Michelle for company, but on a Sunday evening we don't see a big crowd.

"I saw your man today down at the Sonic in Vilonia," she says. For a moment I'm frozen. I know she means The Cop, not Karim. And she doesn't mean it in a bad way, but I don't want to think about The Cop.

"I saw your witch yesterday too," I reply. "Did her divine intervention do you any good?"

Michelle snorts. "The doctor said it might take a year for this thing to heal. She also said I'm supposed to rest as much as I can, but I can't afford that. Rhonda said I could come back full time, but that's before she hired Lisa."

"Don't take this wrong, but I think your doctor's right. I don't think you should be here so much. Maybe it's a good thing that Rhonda's got some extra hands now." Michelle makes a face. "Sorry. I didn't mean it like that."

"None taken, asshole," she laughs.

"I wish you wouldn't call him 'my man,'" I say. "It wasn't like that."

Monday, 20 July

Today I tell Lisa about the first time I got hit on by a customer. I was 18: legal, yes, but young and stupid too—stupid enough to take him up on it. He told me he was recently divorced, and that was a red flag, but I didn't really care much. After my shift he drove me over to his house—one of the ones with beige aluminum siding up toward Friendship Baptist—where we sat on his sectional and started making out.

He was obviously just a good old boy, cute even with his terrible moustache, and we both only wanted to have a good time. But the next thing I knew, there was screaming outside the house, and I looked out the window, and a woman was in a car at the end of the drive screaming at him, "Brian! Whose car is this? What are you doing in there? Don't you care about anything?" and I could see that in her hand she had a gun.

Lisa hoots at this. "Did she shoot at you?" she asks. I am gratified that she finds the story as funny as I do now. At the time I was a little frightened—not so much for myself, but for Brian. But Brian wasn't. He walked out there and talked to her with a gentleness I didn't expect, and calmly took the gun out of her hand, and hugged her. I could see her body shaking with sobs. I guess that part isn't so funny, thinking about it a few years on.

He got in her car and drove her home. I took my cue to leave a few minutes later, and that was the last time I ever made that kind of mistake with a customer. Well, except for The Cop.

I still flirt. We all do, behind the counter. Take the Hostess Guy, for example. Every week without fail he comes in with his little brown shorts, his gleaming smile, his tanned and oddly hairless muscular calves on display, bending over to check the expiry dates on the Ho Hos and the cinnamon buns and the glazed bearclaws and whatnot, reaching up to restock the bread, and all we can do, we girls, is smile and offer him a free sandwich, because to keep him there as long as we can is always our ultimate aim. But he's a once-a-weeker, and a supplier, and we don't even know his name—I mean, we call him Hostess Guy—so flirting works out just fine, a pleasant way to pass the time.

Then there are guys like The Cop, the once- or twice-a-dayers, the ones who sometimes seem to come in just to look you up and down while asking for a pack of smokes. Some of these guys look pretty good, but I always feel beneath them; I am here to serve, and they are here to take. We aren't Hooters or anything; our uniform is, mercifully, a baggy t-shirt and some jeans or shorts, and we're just a bunch of smiling teenage girls, or maybe in our early 20s—that is, we were until Lisa turned up.

And that's a little odd. Why *does* a middle-aged woman want to start a new career in a gas station? It doesn't make

Six Mile Store

sense to me, but I'm glad she's here. It's a slow day, Monday, and it's been only the two of us behind the counter yesterday and today, so we've been talking a lot. She peers at me through her glasses with those small watery blue eyes, and sometimes she's said something, some advice here and there, but as often as not she's been listening.

My own mother—well, when I call her she talks about herself, and it is always a complaint one way or another: a colleague has got a position she wanted, she isn't going to get a raise, her car has sprung some kind of leak or got a flat. A couple of weeks ago I sat on the phone with my mother for a good half hour waiting to tell her my good news—that I had been accepted to that Masters program, and they were going to pay me to come and study and live, and I wouldn't pay a single penny—but she never once asked me a question about what was happening in my life. I'm not sure I even told her about it before we hung up.

Once I start talking to Lisa, though, it turns out I can't stop. I realize that from what I've told her she probably now thinks everybody who comes in this store is creepy or sex-crazed. But it's not true. Most people are friendly and normal, like anywhere.

There is one guy who is my favorite, the nearest to my heart: Darren. Racecar, we call him, because he likes to run stock racing cars. He is good at it, too—always winning competitions, even starting some new circuits up himself. To me, stock car racing just seems like a good excuse to go out drinking in the sunshine with your friends, like Riverfest, but noisier. But you can respect a person's interests. And Racecar takes it seriously. He drives these little cars on the dirt at stupid, deadly speeds, and on his days off he comes in and talks to us and jokes with us like he sees us, like he understands we are real people.

"*Hey Sam Legs, how you feeling?*"

"*Michelle, how's that thumb?*"

"*What are you reading, honey?*"—that last one to me, because I've always got my nose in a book when it's my break time. He acts like he really wants to know, too, but when I ask if he wants to borrow anything, he always says he's not much of a reader.

I know his daughter died a few years ago of meningitis. I was too young to work here then, but I remember seeing a box out collecting for her treatment. I guess she would have been about my age, a little younger, but she went to school in Enola so I didn't know her. "Jessica always liked to read," he'd say, and once he said, "I don't know what your mom and dad are doing, but you let me know if you ever need any help with your books or your fees at that school of yours." I would never take him up on it, of course, but I was touched that he would think of me.

He knew my mom and dad, somehow, in the way everyone out here knows each other, but I wonder how he knew they weren't interested in paying for anything. And he was Rhonda's cousin, a real-life first cousin, not one of these cousins who are really aunts or friends or you don't know how they're really related, if they are at all. And over the years that I've worked here, I've come to think of him as a father, a little—well, more than my own, anyway.

Then, while I'm telling Lisa about all the regulars she'll get to know here, Karim walks right in the door. Yesterday when we were talking about Karim, it never occurred to me that she might get to meet him. He's never been out this way before. I've told him where I work, but he's never come here, never even told me he would. He looks at me in mock surprise, then leans over the counter to give me a kiss. "What are you doing here?" I breathe, delighted.

"I wanted to see where you spend your time without me," he says.

"Want the tour?"

"It's OK," he says. "Just the restroom?"

When he comes out, Karim drops some coins into Amy's kidney transplant box and says I should come to a party at his apartment tonight. "It's Iliyan's name day. You have to come and dance with us." Another kiss, and he's gone as quickly as he arrived.

"So that's Karim," Lisa says. "How long did you say you've been going out with him?"

"A couple of months. It's not serious. He has to go back to Turkey at the end of September," I say, watching his car turn onto the highway.

"But you'd like it to be serious," she says.

I'm silent for a minute, watching the sun winking on Karim's taillights as he disappears around the curve.

"Yes, I really would," I say.

By the time I make it to Karim's apartment, it is packed with more than the usual contingent of Eastern Europeans. Somehow they all knew to be here for Iliyan's party. I see two big ice chests full of PGA punch, and everyone's holding red Solo cups, even the boys drunkenly stumbling through the hora. Stratso and Markar are wailing through an apparently endless klezmer tune on violin and guitar. The carpet was ruined before the boys moved in, so while carelessness isn't exactly encouraged, it also isn't at the forefront of anyone's mind tonight.

Karim is here, too, sitting on the low-slung green sofa behind the coffee table, which is littered with beer bottles, plastic cups, and ashtrays. He's in his socks and bathrobe again, and I wonder if this regular choice of party attire is a mild protest against the near-continual partying he endures in his own home. I sit next to him and snuggle into his warm side. "It was such a nice surprise seeing you at work today," I say.

"How else could I remind you about the party? It was good to come see your place. Maybe I will drop in more now."

"What makes this party different from any of the others?"

"Nothing at all." Karim pulls a tin box of sticky weed out from under the sofa and begins breaking it down, separating the leaves from the stems and seeds. "Roll this for me, baby," he says.

I have developed very few skills in my life, but it's no coincidence that the ones I have mastered are the skills of people who spend a lot of time alone. I can pick basic locks; I can solve a Rubik's cube; I can juggle three balls. And I can roll the finest joints in the central Arkansas area. Karim's joints always run too hot, and he refuses to use a rolling machine; I learned a long time ago how to roll mine upside down.

"What are you going to do when you've gone back to Turkey? Who is going to roll your joints for you?" I ask, packing the weed down—not too tight, not too loose. "You're going to waste so much bud." I smile at him as I lick the paper, then tear the excess away.

"I talked to my advisor in Turkey. He is happy with the work I'm doing here. It may be that I don't go this September."

"You're staying?" My heart starts to pound; even the music starts to go faster, the dancing boys whirling and tripping each other up. Everyone is laughing, and I feel high, though we haven't lit the joint yet.

"I don't know. Maybe we make the best of it until I know, OK?"

Iliyan appears next to me. "Hey, happy birthday, man," I say, giving him a hug and handing him the joint. "Here's your present."

He laughs. "Thanks, but it's not my birthday, it's my name day. Today, I'm a saint," he says, sparking up and taking a deep drag. The glow from the lit end briefly illuminates his face, accentuating the handsome Slavic angles of his jaw and cheekbones, and I can't help but agree—he looks heavenly.

"Hey, you know, Iliyan is a saint to me too. Actually he's like an angel," Karim says. "This room is full of saints and angels. *Opa!*" Karim gets up from the sofa and joins the dancers briefly, flashing his bare legs, navigating the dance until he reaches one of the ice chests. He fills three cups with punch and begins weaving his way back to the sofa.

"What kind of saint are you?" I ask Iliyan.

"I'm a fallen one," he says, passing the joint back to me. "Like you."

Tuesday, 21 July

"There's a man out there filling up a whole bunch of gas cans," I tell Sam Legs. She's squatting under the counter, sorting bills into color-coded envelopes and feeding that money into the safe that sits underneath the cash register. She stands and looks out the window.

"Oh, it's them," she says.

The bell above the door tinkles as a young family walks in. The mother is wearing a long, faded dress and carrying a fussy baby wearing only a diaper. Five more children, ranging in ages from 3 to 10, accompany her in silence. Each child is wearing clothing that is clearly old and well-mended, but clean.

The mother hands the eldest child some cash. "Go pick you something," she says. The children walk to the candy aisle, while the mother disappears to the back of the store. The father walks in. He is shirtless, but otherwise dressed in jeans and work boots. His hair and beard are long but groomed.

"How many slabs of bacon you got?" he asks me.

Six Mile Store

I look into the meat fridge. "Well, we have three here," I say.

"I'll take 'em all," he says.

"You want all three slabs of bacon?"

"Yes ma'am. Y'all got any more in back there in the cooler?"

Sam Legs jumps in. "Nah, we just got what's here."

"I can go look," I say, but Sam Legs shakes her head.

"It's empty back there. We have a meat delivery coming next week."

"Three'll do me for now," the man says, then goes to join the woman at the back.

"I'm pretty sure there's more bacon back there," I whisper to Sam Legs.

"Trust me," she says. "I'll tell you later." She begins weighing up the slabs of bacon, carefully wrapping each in a broad swathe of white waxed paper, then writing the weight and price onto each parcel in Sharpie.

The children walk silently to the counter. They each place one candy bar on the counter. "Is this enough?" the biggest one asks me, holding out a five dollar bill.

"Yes, that's plenty, thank you, sweetheart." I ring up the candy bars and hand the girl the change.

"Thank you, ma'am," she whispers. Each child takes a candy bar and stands to the side. Sam Legs ferries the wrapped bacon parcels to the register as the mom and dad walk up. The father is carrying a stack of eight packages of disposable diapers. The mother carries the baby in one hand, and in the other she holds a canvas bag that she has packed full of hygiene items: razors, toothpaste, toothbrushes, baby powder, shampoo, soap, and baby lotion.

"I can get y'all over here," Sam Legs says.

"We had $150 on gasoline," the man says. "Hey, I heard y'all have a new lady working here. I heard it's my cousin Lisa. Is she here?"

"Yeah, she's in the back," I reply, bagging up the diapers while Sam Legs rings up the rest of the family's purchases.

"Would you mind to ask her to come out and say hi? I ain't seen her in a while," he says, heaving the wrapped slabs of bacon onto his shoulders, then walking out the door.

I walk to the office and poke my head around the door. "Hey, Lisa, your cousin is here. He wants to say hi." Lisa looks up from the paperwork Rhonda's got her working on. The office is a mess, full of cash bags and papers strewn everywhere. This is only Lisa's third day here, but she's already created a lot of chaos in this office. I guess she's got a lot to sort out, since Rhonda hasn't been able to work for a while.

"My cousin?" she says, getting up and heading out. I notice she's careful to lock the office door, which is a good idea. You can't see the office door from the registers, and you never know if one of the customers might decide to peek in and see what they can see. There are a lot of poor folks around here who might be tempted by those cash bags, though really they shouldn't be out at all unless we're going directly to the bank. I make a mental note to remind Lisa about that.

As Lisa goes out to talk to the man, I see each child is holding a bag of diapers and standing by the back of their battered orange pickup truck. The man loads the older children and the groceries into the truck's open bed, alongside the gas cans. He turns to Lisa. I can't hear what they're saying, but he looks serious.

"What in Sam Hill was that?" I ask.

Sam Legs shakes her head. "I ain't seen them in months."

"I've never seen them. Who are they?"

"That's them Woodards. Rhonda says they live up there in the woods near Palarm Creek. Their daddy's some kinda prepper out there. Those kids don't see other kids cause their momma homeschools them. They keep everything they need, and they come out here once in a blue moon to stock up. Rhonda told her one time they could get some of this stuff cheaper up there at Harps, but she said they don't go out that far. Anyway, you can't tell them we got more bacon or they'll take every last bit of it. They live on it all year long."

I watch as the mother, father, and baby climb into the cab of the truck. They head off up Saltillo way. Lisa looks a little red in the face as she starts back toward the store.

"Those kids were nice, though," I say. "Not like some who come in here."

"I reckon they'll get their ass beat if they act up," Sam Legs says. "Hey, Lisa, I didn't know you had kin out here," she says as Lisa comes back in.

"We ain't close," Lisa says. She goes back into the office and shuts the door behind her.

The Cop was handsome, for sure. Still is. For a little while last year he came in regularly when I was on shift—he knew which car was mine—and he sometimes just came in to get a drink and have a chat. I was flattered and confused; he was definitely twice my age, but gosh, he was good-looking.

A. M. Belsey

We all knew him, of course, because of what happened with Rhonda when she got sick, and just because everybody knows everybody out here. So I knew he wasn't married, and he looked at me with a steadiness I had never seen before. It was like he was putting a collar around my neck and attaching a leash. So I flirted, the way I flirt with almost everyone, but I gave him a special smile, and made sure I was the one to serve him when he came to the counter. Even Sam Legs noticed, and she was often in the clouds about these things.

What happened the night I came *around* the counter after a late shift, though—well, that changed everything. When I think about it, it doesn't feel like a memory. It feels like it's happening to me right now.

I mention to him one Sunday afternoon that I'll be the one closing up that night, expecting him to come in for a chat when it's quiet and we're closing down. I'm surprised, then, that he doesn't come in like he usually does. But when I finish my final lock-up and emerge into the honeysuckle-scented spring evening, he's standing at the back of the store, where it's dark, with only fields and woods around, and the abandoned Fischer house hunkering down empty and lonely across the road. When I walk back to greet him, he corners me—pushing me up against the back wall of the store, taking both of my hands and pressing them against the cold aluminium siding.

"Are you going to be mine?" he says.

"Ahhhh," I breathe, looking at him with what I hope is a frank directness. There's no moon tonight, but it looks like the whole sky is reflected in his dark blue eyes.

Six Mile Store

"Because if you're mine, you're mine. Nobody else's." He tightens his hands around my wrists as he says that, and I get butterflies in my stomach.

I laugh a little and reply, "Well, I'm not going to let you handcuff me, if that's what you mean," attempting an impertinent grin.

He doesn't smile back. He looks at me hard, and presses against me more firmly than before. As I squirm in protest, I feel his crotch stiff against my hip. He leans in, mouth close to my ear, and whispers, "Oh, you will. You'll do whatever I say. I told you. If you're mine, you're *mine*."

He grips my wrists with such force that I imagine an electric current running through me and into the metal siding behind me. My heart begins to race—now more from fear than desire—and any warmth that had been left in the evening air seems to have dissipated, leaving me chilled and shaking. I suddenly realize that I don't know this man, really. I don't know what he's capable of doing to me.

I appeal to his sense of propriety. "Please don't do this here. I'm at work. What if someone drives past and sees us?"

He smirks. "You act so innocent, but I know you're hiding something. There's a wildness in you, girl, and I think I'm the only one who can unleash it." He leans in further to kiss me, but I shift away as much as I can. His hands release my wrists; he begins pulling at my shirt hem, my waistband. "Don't fight me," he whispers, his breath ragged on my neck.

I wriggle out from under him. "Don't do this," I say, with conviction. To my surprise, he stops still for a moment, then he raises his hands and backs up a few steps. I walk as steadily as I can to my car, heart pounding in my ears, and I drive home via a route I have never taken before—though of course he already knows exactly where I live.

Since then I've treated him like any old customer. I don't know if he's confused by my apparent change of heart, but I don't want to answer any of his questions if he is. He still comes in; I try to avoid seeing him if I can, and if I can't, I pretend I've never met him before. I don't tell the other girls what happened.

Today he comes in, goes to the fountain, mixes up a suicide. I see that the slicer needs to be cleaned, so I take it apart and start washing the blade guard in the steel sink. Sam Legs takes the hint and stands at the counter with a smile. "Is that all for you?"

"It's all for now. I came in to ask if anyone's been here acting funny, meeting up in the back lot or anything," he says. I am probably imagining it, but I feel like his eyes are burning into the back of my neck.

"Not that I've seen. What's going on?" Out of the corner of my eye I can see Sam Legs holding his cash up to the light, like a cop is going to be passing us bad bills.

"Some of the boys down at Vilonia school got caught with some pot in their lockers a couple of months ago," he says. "They barely got to graduate. The school board asked us to figure out who's dealing around here. We've been working on a few leads. Seems like this is a pretty good meet-up spot to me. Pretty private around the back." I know that last sentence is directed at me, but I don't acknowledge I've heard anything.

Six Mile Store

I try to ignore them both. I squeeze out the sponge and start scrubbing on the slicer's blade, careful not to nick my fingers. Michelle isn't the only one who's been injured by this thing. I've got my own little scar from tangling with it on my left ring finger, right near the nail.

I could probably tell him who some of the local dealers are—hell, I can't imagine he doesn't already know. One of the houses near my parents nearly burned down a few months ago when someone's meth lab caught fire. I figure this conversation is his excuse for standing around making me feel uncomfortable.

"Nobody hangs out here," Sam Legs says. "Mostly they just gas up and go, unless they're eating their lunch. I never saw anyone acting weird."

"Well, girls, keep your eyes open for me." I hear the bell tinkle as he goes out the door. I don't know if he looks back; I'm using a paper towel to buff up the blade before reassembling the slicer.

"You ain't talking to him anymore?" Sam Legs asks me.

"Oh, did I tell you Karim came in?" I say. "He showed up yesterday afternoon. Lisa got to meet him."

"Oh yeah, of course, you've got all them foreign boys now."

"Not *all* of them! I'm not that lucky."

"Well, live it up, girl. There won't be anyone interesting at that new place you're going."

"Don't forget I'll still be here at the weekends," I remind her. "Hey, maybe a couple of rich doctors will come in looking for directions to Greers Ferry and take us both away from all this."

"I've had enough of doctors, thank you."

Lisa walks out of the office. "Rhonda told me to make sure these shelves are dusted and fronted," she says, disappearing into the pet food aisle. Nobody likes that job, so even Sam Legs has to admit there are some good things about having Lisa here.

"Hey Lisa, when you're done I'll show you how to bag up the ice," Sam Legs says, looking at me with a smirk. If there's one job worse than prettifying the shelves, it's packing up 10-pound bags of ice. It's a hotter and dirtier job than you'd imagine, and this time of year we have to keep up with it. A few weeks ago I spent the whole Friday night and all of my shift on Saturday just scooping ice into bags, twirling them shut, loading them into a shopping cart, and heaving them into the outdoor cooler. Everybody and their daddy had to have a Fourth of July party. My arms were sore for the whole next week.

The rest of my shift passes without incident. Shirley comes in to ask for cigarettes and glare at us. Billy Wayne walks over wearing just his cutoff shorts and yellow hard hat. I slip him that quarter I owe him; he doesn't notice. Racecar tells Sam Legs an off-color joke about a man who offers to replace some woman's rooster. I pilfer some banana Laffy Taffy, which works as well as anything else to help my dull headache from last night disappear, and by the time I drive home and fall alone into my bed I feel, if not happy, at least content in the knowledge that my life is shaping up into something a little less liminal.

Thursday, 3 September

My advisor, Dr Vowan, starts by asking if we can say a prayer; I know how to form the basics of a prayer in my mouth, but some men can get funny about women taking the lead. I'm not sure what he means by "we." He glances at me, so I take a calculated risk and simply lower my eyes in silence. He clears his throat and begins, "Dear God, we just come to you here in the name of Jesus, Lord..."

As he prays that God will *just* look down on us, Lord, *just* bless us here in this place, *just* be with us, God, I peek around the room. Everything is new. The carpet is royal blue with footprints in it; the chair I sit in is wide and low, upholstered in a scratchy but otherwise pristine green and blue plaid wool that matches the curtains. The desk is pine, with an incongruous green leather top, and it looks like it was built yesterday; the leather is shiny and unmarked. The white walls stretch around the room, empty of books or any other decoration apart from a framed diploma hanging on the wall behind his desk, declaring him Greg Vowan, Doctor of Ministry. It was awarded by Oral Roberts

University. A dark smudge mars the lower left of the gilt frame.

This building, and specifically this office, had to be redecorated after the siege last year, when Damien Lord, a mature student, barricaded himself in the administrative building with his fledgling cult—twenty-three Pentecostal girls who claimed to be his sister-wives. The handful who were eventually dragged out alive after the shootings and the fire said they believed he was a prophet and a warrior. He was going to be their divine champion at Armageddon, which they all claimed was imminent.

Behind me, I know the office door is ajar; Dr Vowan explained when I met him in July that for propriety he never sits alone in a closed room with a woman who isn't his wife or daughter. As he says Amen, I murmur along noncommittally, raising my head and sneaking a quick look at the family photo angled slightly toward me on his desk. The higher the hair, the closer to God, they say.

"First, Dr. Vowan, I want to say thanks so much for this opportunity to teach here and earn my MA at the same time," I start, but he interrupts.

"Let me just stop you there," he says. "We know your educational background, and while on paper you may qualify for this program, I'm personally a little concerned about the influence you may bring with you from that more, ahh, secular institution. So we're going to start you with seniors taking electives, on a trial basis for now."

I feel my face start to flush. Seniors at this college are primarily men, many of them older students. I will be teaching men older than I am. This wasn't the plan we had discussed in July, but I know not to make a fuss, so I keep quiet and wait.

"Well? Do you think that's a fair assessment of the problems we might have with you?" he asks, eyes glittering darkly under thick eyebrows.

"Ah, well, I hope you won't have any problems with me," I reply, smiling inanely, trying to look small and a little stupid, like I couldn't be a threat to anyone. "And I think it's great that I will be teaching elective classes. That means the students will be really interested in the material rather than taking it because they ha–"

"All of our students want to learn," Dr. Vowan interjects. "They're here to learn, not to play around. These are serious, dedicated men and women, expanding their minds to the glory of God. You should try to remember that," he says, standing up. "I'll see you the same time next week. In the meantime, bring me your lesson plan for our approval," he continues, opening the cracked door a little wider and ushering me out.

Leaving the lobby I walk straight into the glare of the low autumn sun, blinded for a moment, with a sudden shocking headache throbbing right behind my eyes.

Heading back to my dorm, I take in the uninspired architecture: insipid beige paint accenting over-square brick buildings with flat roofs. The regular rectangles of pale grass between the crisscrossing sidewalks are spongy and overgroomed. There are no mature trees anywhere; all of the older buildings on campus had been torn down and replaced in the 1980s, and landscaping now consists of

Bradford pears and young birches dotted around at regular intervals.

My building, my new home, had escaped the administration's improvement drive, making it one of the oldest buildings at the college. Its dark wood floors and wood-paneled walls feel dignified and ancient in comparison to the bland modernity that dominated the rest of the campus. My room has space for a bed and desk and mini-fridge and not much else, but I have my own shower room and sink—not huge, but at least I don't have to share shower facilities with my potential students.

Except they aren't my potential students anymore. Pretty much the only women who stay in the dorms are the freshers; the rest either get married and move in with their husbands or drop out long before they reach their senior year.

I lie down on my hard little bed and consider my problem. Is it a problem, really? After all, no matter what Vowan says, I will be teaching people who have already decided to take English Literature as an elective, not just those who are focused on finishing their Bible degrees. The more I think about it, the more I like the idea. Serious, dedicated men. Maybe some women. I start drafting a plan.

The atmosphere at Karim's that night is frenetic, with violins and clarinets wailing and moaning, sliding around each other in the air, mingling with the fragrance of incense and marijuana and spicy food. Everything looks soft and blue in the dim light, with lava lamps in the corners and blacklights shining on psychedelic posters.

I notice Markar is kissing a girl I've seen here a couple of times. She's pretty: tall, green eyes, wavy hair, melodic laugh. I wonder if they are a couple now, and if they will stay together—if she and I will get to know each other, maybe eventually be friends. It has been a long time since I had a girl friend, let alone one who is already part of this twilight world suffused with pot and klezmer. Trying to explain its appeal to anyone else, especially anyone else I'm likely to meet in my new job, would be futile.

Karim takes me to his bare, quiet room, the only light the rising moon glimmering through his window. We stand for a moment, not moving or talking, just looking at each other. Then I unbutton his shirt. I sit on his little twin bed and rest my cheek on his taut stomach. "When do you find out how long you're staying?" I ask.

"Good news. I found out today. I'm staying an extra year, *aşkım*."

I feel lightheaded. I pull him down to join me on the bed, run my hands over his stomach and sides and chest, kiss his lips and neck and shoulders. He feels warm and dangerous and incongruously soft. I don't want to stop touching him, my white hand on his dark skin fluorescing in the dim light. Laughing, he rolls over to his bedside table to grab a joint that is waiting there. He lights it and hands it to me. For a moment I consider suggesting that we go back in with the others to celebrate, but then he leans in for a blowback and everything becomes a whirling and beautiful confusion, and we are lost in our own dance.

Friday, 4 September

Around 1 am, I make it back to my dormitory only to find that it is locked. It's dark out here, even with that almost full moon now hanging high in the sky. A dim porch light barely illuminates the heavy door to the building. The late summer air is humid, furry in my throat, and mosquitoes loom.

I have a key to my room, but not to the dormitory building itself. I can see my window, just one floor up from where I stand, next to a sturdy-looking 1930s cast iron drain pipe affixed to the solid red brick. I consider whether I am straight enough to climb up, break the glass, deal with the aftermath the next day. But the maple saplings would be too young and slender to be of any use at all even if they were nearer the building, and I don't think I want to risk scaling the sheer face of the brick.

Out of the corner of my eye I catch some movement in the lobby. Peeking through the glass panel in the door, I see a young woman in red pajamas taking a Coke out of the vending machine. I open my bag and pull out my ID badge. I knock, holding my badge close to the glass so she can see that I'm a fellow student, not a threat.

The woman doesn't seem startled. She looks up at the door, then glances up the hall quickly before she heads over to open it for me. She glares at me from under overlong black bangs. "What are you doing?" she hisses. "Curfew is 11pm! Your RA is going to murder you."

"I don't have... I mean, I'm an MA student. Well, *the* MA student, I guess? Working with Dr. Vowan? I'm like a student teac..."

"Shut up and go into your room or we'll both get expelled," she whispers with a glare before stalking off to the opposite hallway from mine. I take her advice.

The next morning at breakfast in the cafeteria I see the girl from the lobby again. She looks tired. I don't say anything as I approach her table and plop down across from her.

"It's you," she says flatly.

I give her a bright smile. "Good morning! Thanks for letting me in last night. By the way, why were you in the lobby so late yourself?"

She sighs. "It's a long story. I have a lot of studying to do. Be glad it was me; anyone else would have dragged you to the RA."

"Why didn't you?"

She shrugs. "I don't really care what anyone else does. I mind my own business."

I take that as a hint not to ask any more questions. But then she starts to talk, then stops herself.

"What?" I ask.

"I wondered if you might have been out, you know, partying. Your eyes were a dead giveaway."

"I thought you said you mind your own business."

"Forget it," she replies. "Just remember you're not totally alone here." She stands, picking up her tray. "I'm Kim. I'll see you in Lit, I guess." She strides off, shoving her tray into the rack with the rest of the empties, then flicking her long black hair off her shoulders as she leaves the building.

Intrigued, I finish my coffee and muffin and rush out of the cafeteria toward the Cleburne Arts building, the newest facility on campus. When I met up with Vowan in July, he took me on a brief, eerie tour of Cleburne: no furniture, no decoration, just white walls under white lights, with the chilly, fishy smell of an enthusiastic new HVAC system permeating the entire structure. As I enter the building again, I notice not much has changed since that visit, except that it's now very hot.

"...electrical problems in the air conditioning system..." A woman I vaguely recognize from the administration building strides past me, leading a man in blue overalls through the hall. She looks worried and skeletal, though any aesthetic shortcomings she has are almost certainly exacerbated by the harsh fluorescent lighting. As I approach the door to the lecture hall, I notice that one of the tubes, though ostensibly new, is already flickering.

I walk up to the door and, through the panes, notice Kim talking to Vowan. He is scowling. She takes something from him, puts it in her pocket. I push the door open; at the sound of the creaking hinges—why are these new hinges making any noise?—they spring apart.

Surely they're not involved with each other. I think back to the blonde with big bangs pictured on Vowan's desk—a very different type of woman from the dark, gamine Kim. But some men don't have a type, or, for some, just "young" is type enough. And—here he was, alone in a room, door shut, with a woman who is not his... I have paused for only a moment, but that is long enough to have been overtaken by students who have begun filing in.

Vowan's literature class is more diverse in appearance than I had expected. After the Damien Lord incident, which made international headlines, I knew the college went on a PR counter-attack, spreading the good news that Conway, Arkansas—population 27,000, set in a dry county, with plenty of parking, about 200 churches in the area if you're Protestant and even one if you're not, and a 24-hour Wal-Mart—is a great place for young Christian students of all sorts, not *necessarily* fundamentalists, to come and honor god through their educational pursuits. And maybe it helps that this Baptist college is accredited, unlike the Bob Joneses of the world. But, as the students enter the lecture hall, I can't help but be surprised to see that nearly half are women, and over half of those women are wearing trousers.

When class begins, Vowan introduces me as an MA student who will be teaching some of his classes this term. I see the students sizing me up: blue jeans, short-ish hair, traces of last night's makeup. I'm not one of them, at least in the ways they think are important. Still, I feel confident that we can find common ground through the syllabus I've been thinking about: start with ideas they're familiar with, expand on them, get them thinking. They're serious students; they want to learn.

Kim is staring a hole through me, too, from the center of the lecture hall. I endure the rest of the class, desperate to know what is going on between her and Vowan. When he dismisses us, I think she gets lost in the crowd moving through the creaking doors, but—there she is, waiting for me.

"So are you going to tell me what that was?" I ask, not looking directly at Kim, though we are walking together out of the building.

"What did you see?"

"I saw y'all jump apart like you'd been scalded. Are you and him a thing?"

Kim laughs. "Him? He's so ugly he'd scare a buzzard off a gut pile. Anyway, I'm going to the library. Seeya." She veers off to a concrete bunker-like facility that had recently replaced the previous library: a hobbit-hole dug out in the late 1960s, which had been found unsuitable for the long-term storage of books thanks to a tendency toward damp. The new library bunker has separate men's and women's study carrels: women to the left, men to the right. It's hard to picture Kim there.

Saturday, 5 September

Tinkle, tinkle. I turn with my usual "hey," then realize it's Rhonda hobbling in, looking even grayer than usual. She is sweating. "Rhonda, my god," I say, running around the counter. She looks like she is going to faint.

"Darren, he flipped. Darren flipped," Rhonda gasps. I stare at her. Darren? Flipped?

"What are you saying, Rhonda?" I've heard of people flipping out, shooting their wives and kids, shooting themselves, but Darren?

"In his car, he flipped. He fell on his head. He might be dead. Oh god!" Rhonda sits right in the middle of the floor, just as Michelle comes out of the cooler.

"Rhonda, what is going on!" Michelle runs up to us, looking panicked

"Michelle—lock the door for a second. We need to get Rhonda to the office." I heave her up—my god, her body feels like a sack of feed, and I can haul plenty these days, but she can't weigh more than 70 pounds. I can feel her collarbone pressing into my arms as I half pull, half push her back to the office, leaving Michelle looking for a sharpie to write a "Be back soon!" note for the door. I think too late to remind her to turn the pumps off—but never mind, we can get there if we hear knocking.

I shove Rhonda down into her desk chair, pushing some of Lisa's chaos of papers off the center of the desk so she can rest her head on her arms. They fall all over the floor. The sweat is dripping off Rhonda's *ears*, for heaven's sake. "Rhonda, why did you walk over here?"

"I couldn't stay there," she says, muffled by her sleeves. "I had to come, I had to say." Her body shakes with sobs.

We eventually get enough details to understand the basics. Darren—Racecar Darren, my Darren!—had been at a meet when something went wrong with one of his tires. His car flipped over, and now he's in Conway Regional with a terrible injury, or maybe dead, or maybe his injury isn't so terrible—it's hard to know because, with Rhonda only a cousin, nobody will give her information over the phone.

"You enjoying your new place?"

I don't want to think about how he knows I've moved. "It's a good opportunity to finish my education and save some money." I try to be as non-committal as I can. "So what's going on with Darren?"

Rhonda is back home. After Michelle went over with her and got her tucked up in bed, she called The Cop to see if he could give us some answers, and of course he came down here instead of just talking to her.

"Well, he's in an induced coma right now. They did some surgery to reduce pressure on his brain. When he wakes up they'll do some tests. They can't say what damage might have been done."

"But they expect him to wake up?"

"Yeah. He was breathing on his own when he went in. Wasn't talking, but seemed to understand enough to move his arms and legs. But there's a bleed on the brain that's a real worry."

"Well. Thank you for coming in here to let us know."

"So what are you studying over there?"

I sigh. "I'm doing a Masters in Literature."

"What's your favorite book?"

"I don't know. Probably *As I Lay Dying*. Maybe not the best title to discuss right now."

He raises an eyebrow. "You don't know? I like Faulkner. Good old boy."

"That's certainly the image he cultivated, yes."

"Any crazy campus hijinks you want to tell me about?"

My advisor is having an affair with a girl in my dorm. I don't say that, of course. What I actually say is, "At a Baptist college? Not really."

"Why are you such a hard nut to crack these days?"

"Just busy. Thanks again for coming in."

"OK, OK, I get the picture." He goes to the cooler, comes back with a Mountain Dew. His radio bleeps, a garbled female voice dispatching all available cars to a code something or other. "Gotta dash. See you later, honey."

Thursday, 10 September

Vowan reciting his opening prayer, the door cracked open behind me, the wool chair itching the backs of my knees, my eyes restlessly flitting around the soulless room—I wonder if this weekly experience will become a touchstone, something I will always remember when I think about this time in my life. Over the past week I've been observing Vowan's teaching practices and his preferences, the way he interacts with his students, where his patience begins and ends.

"Now. Your lesson plan?"

I've been excited about sharing this idea with Vowan, if a little apprehensive given the scope and the potential risk. "I thought of something the students might like. These metaphysical poets, Andrew Marvell and so on, used a lot of religious imagery in their poems. I think I might use religion as a foundation to get them talking about what it means when..."

"Yes, yes, that sounds possible. Good job on honoring your students' commitment to God. They'll appreciate that."

"OK, and you know the metaphysicals were logical and philosophical too, right? And some of their imagery..."

"Yes, yes, beautiful poems. I remember John Donne. Great plan, great plan." I haven't had a chance to continue, to explain that some of the interpretations I want to look at may challenge our students. But Vowan goes on.

"I need to finish up now. If you see Kim Anders, could you let her know I've got that book she wanted to borrow?"

Later on, I do see Kim walking across campus, heading to the atrium, where I know she's going to get a Coke and some Fritos from the machine and sit and read a textbook. I've watched her do it every afternoon now, without fail. Today I surprise her, slide in next to her before she can object.

"Hey there," I whisper. She looks up, makes a face. I go on: "Girl, do you really hate me that much? I never see you talking to anyone else."

"It's not that." She stops, sighs. "I just have so much work to do. I have to graduate this year, keep my grades up. I have to study."

"Not all the time, though."

"Yes. All the time. I have a scholarship and I can't let my grades slip. But the words just fall out of my head. Unless I..." She stops. I notice her pupils are dilated. She seems a little flushed.

"Vowan told me to tell you he's got the book you wanted to borrow."

At that she lets out a little snort. "He's not lending me a book. He's got something else for me. You know what I mean?"

"Are you telling me you're sleeping with Vowan to keep your grades up? Is that what's going on?"

"No!" A couple of heads turn toward us from the TV area, where some freshmen are watching tennis. "No," she repeats, whispering this time. "But he helps me. He's been selling me Ritalin. I take it so I can focus on my work. It helps so much."

I laugh. "Girl, I wish you'd told me before! What's he charging you? I can probably get you a better deal. I know someone."

"Aşkım, I have to tell you something."

I'm lying in Karim's bed, shivering naked under the sheet. Unlike the Cleburne Arts building, the air conditioning isn't broken here. Quite the opposite.

"That sounds serious."

"Well, it is a little serious. I have to tell you I did something." He looks forlorn, almost heartbroken. Before I can ask what has happened, he continues: "Before I met you, I had a woman, another woman. And then for a while I see both of you."

I sit for a few seconds with my feelings, trying to get a handle on what this revelation means for me, for us as a couple. If I were to be completely honest with Karim, I would have to admit there has been some overlap with him and Lynn, too, but only in a sexual sense. Nothing emotional, no relationship. But I don't feel compelled to share any of that information. "When did you stop seeing her?"

"Months ago, aşkım, I swear it. I see her in maybe July. We talked on the phone after. But nothing else."

Six Mile Store

I'm struck then by a flash of guilt. The last time I slept with Lynn was also July, that night we had a huge fight. We haven't really spoken much since then. I decide that this is ultimately something I can handle. Still, I need to know one thing. "Karim, please don't worry. In July we had known each other for just a couple of months. And we hadn't made any promises then. You thought you would be back in Turkey by now. But...is she someone I know?"

"No! No. She is someone from my work."

"Your school?"

"Yes, my school. She is not there now. Maybe she dropped out. I have lost her phone number. I don't see her now. I swear it, *aşkım*. I swear it."

Monday, 16 November

I'm walking back to my shitty little dorm, Vowan's words echoing in my mind. *There have been a number of complaints from my students. Obviously you can't teach this class any longer. Expect a clarification about next steps within a couple of weeks.*

The brief whoop of a police siren interrupts my whirring thoughts. I turn. The Cop.

"Why are you here?"

"I got a report I need to check out. Heard there's some shady stuff happening over here."

"On *this* campus? You sure you got the right place?" I know what I know, but I'm not telling The Cop anything if I can help it.

"Oh yeah. Maybe you can walk me over to the administration building?"

"I'm sure you can find your way around. See you later." I start to walk off.

"Wait, honey, please." I stop. The Cop goes on. "I feel like maybe a door closed between us somehow. How am I going to open it up again?"

Six Mile Store

"You're not. I have a boyfriend. There's no door between us now because there was nothing between us before."

"A boyfriend, really? What's he like?"

I consider what I can tell him about Karim: his dressing gown, his strong cigarettes, the *çiğ köfte*, the spicy perfume he gave me? For weeks I've been repeating the same things to myself: it can't last; he can't stay forever, it can't be a real relationship. And yet, and yet, and yet, back I go.

"He's kind. He respects me. He doesn't force me to do anything." I look hard at The Cop. He doesn't acknowledge my implication.

"*Aşkım*, do you have a passport? I wonder if you would like to see Turkey."

It's evening. With no desire to be on campus tonight after that scorched-earth meeting with Vowan, I've come to stay with Karim in his little bedroom, something I rarely do thanks to the cramped twin bed. The Bulgarian boys are having a quiet jam session in the living room, playing a gentle tune that's winding itself through sadness and joy, yearning and resolution, and then back through it all again, endlessly.

I'm in my pajamas, sitting on that little bed, helping him fold his laundry. He stacks our piles on the dresser as we go; side-by-side, it's apparent that his work is much neater than mine. I try to copy his methods but he's too fast. His orderliness appeals to the child in me who was never given the gift of direction.

"I would love to see Turkey. But I don't have a passport yet. I'll get one."

"It's easy to get one, *aşkım*. I say do it now, why not? Maybe one day in spring I take you to see Cappadocia. The hot air balloons. Then my mother will try to fatten you up."

Travel to another country seems impossible, a dream I've never thought could be more than that until now. But I make some notes in my head: find my birth certificate, get a passport, save up some money, just in case. Next summer maybe I can take a couple of weeks off.

"Do I need fattening?" I ask.

Karim smiles, the corners of his eyes crinkling. He reaches toward me, cups my cheek with his hand, runs his thumb over my lips. I hear an oboe dance through a precise little embellishment "You are perfect, *aşkım*." His fingertips brush down my neck, shoulder, arm. He takes the towel I was folding and puts it back into the unfolded laundry, adds his dressing gown to the pile, then shoves the whole thing to the end of the bed. He grasps my shoulders and presses my body back toward his pillows, kissing my ear, the corners of my mouth, my neck. He's leaning on one arm, but his lower body is on mine, and I can feel his hardness against my thigh as he inches his free hand up my pajama top. Not encountering the usual bra seems to excite him further, his hot breath in my ear as he cups and caresses my breast, fingering my hardening nipple.

Karim begins whispering to me in Turkish, phrases I don't know yet, though I think I hear "nobody else" and "mine." I watch his bronze hand move over my white stomach, then under the waistband of my shorts, and I catch my breath as his fingers find my own urgency. Kissing me hard, now, he moves his fingers into me, stroking me with his thumb. Within me I can feel a mounting heat, an aching storm of pleasure beginning to coalesce, all while Karim moves with growing agitation: teeth nipping at my lips, head nudging my neck, whispering things I don't understand with cracked breathlessness.

Karim has always been generous but has never denied himself pleasure for too long, so I am not surprised when he tugs down my shorts—but this time he pushes me upward and bows his head between my legs. I watch as he runs the tip of his tongue over me, my pale thighs framing his brown curls, then my own head falls back in an exquisite agony as be begins to tongue me firmly, his fingers moving inside me, for what feels like an hour, or a few seconds, until I climax so strongly that I can hardly make a sound at all, legs shaking, body heaving.

Only then does Karim break contact with me for a moment, to put a condom on, and I find that my body needs him, that it feels lonely and incomplete without his touch. But I'm made whole again when he maneuvers his body next to mine, then under mine, as I guide him into me and we start to move together. I've never experienced a second climax so closely after a first, and I'm surprised how, if a first orgasm is like a flash of lightning, a repeat is like a rumble of thunder that goes on and on, as my nipple crushes gently between my lover's teeth, and my body rubs greedily against his.

It's too much for Karim, too, who has now begun to moan, pleading wordlessly for release. So I lean over him, moving my hips in a way that allows him to decide his own movement and intensity. It takes only a few moments: I feel him convulse as he whimpers an obscenity in Turkish—this one I do know. And for a moment we are still.

"What on earth were you saying to me before?" I ask a few moments later, in a breathless laugh.

"I say, 'I want you to be mine forever. And for no other man to touch your pussy, ever.' This kind of thing."

I consider. "It sounds better in Turkish," I finally reply.

"Yes, well," he says, "anyway, it's true."

Tuesday, 1 December

I can't stop myself sobbing while driving over to Karim's house, having shoved that wretched letter into my bag to show him. Vowan is kicking me out of my job and the program altogether. I've got nothing. I'm going back to nothing.

Blue lights stretch around the corner as I approach Karim's place, and when I see his front door is open and the police are going in and out, I stop breathing for a second. I park up and get out.

"What's going on?" I ask.

"Drug bust," says one of the cops. I look past his shoulder and see a group of people wearing gloves, one carrying a camera—and, with an electric shock, I notice The Cop watching the raid, apparently in a supervisory capacity. "You live near here?" he goes on.

"Yeah, just a nosy neighbor," I reply, trying to laugh a little, look unperturbed, keep my head turned half away so The Cop doesn't see me too. Inside I'm screaming. Karim isn't a drug user, apart from cigarettes, alcohol, a little bit of pot, like all of us. This kind of police presence seems unwarranted for a guy with a baggie of marijuana. Of course, though—he's Turkish. He's not like everyone else. He's suspicious.

I drive to my dorm and get on the phone, but I can't get through to Lynn. His deadbeat roommate isn't home I guess, or maybe he's too stoned or hungover to pick up.

I try to call my parents for the first time in forever. I feel like I could use their advice, even though they have never given it to me. My father answers. "Oh, it's you. Want to talk to your mom?" he says, then immediately puts the phone on the table. I hear him yelling "Janie, it's for you." I can hear the sound of a sports event on the television behind him. I wait a long time for my mother to pick up the phone.

"Well, it's been a while," she says. "I didn't even get a chance to tell you what Debra got up to at the office. She is such a little bitch. She put the supply information into the spreadsheet wrong, and then you know of course who got blamed for it? Well, I just wasn't going to stand for it. I said, Charlie, I said, now this ain't my fault and you know it. You know I ain't gonn—"

I hang up silently, pressing the little knobs without making a click, closing the connection. I hold them down for a good two minutes, to make sure I don't accidentally reopen the call when I put the handset back in the cradle. I wonder how long it will take her to notice I'm not on the line anymore. I could have easily sat there for 10 minutes without saying a word, listening to her go on about herself.

I wonder if she will call back. It seems unlikely. She never does.

Six Mile Store

I look around my room and wonder why I am in it. Where can I go now?

Friday, 4 December

I finally got in touch with Lynn's roommate yesterday. He told me what happened, and where to come. So now I'm here at the Faulkner County Jail, sitting across from Lynn on a pathetic little bench, separated from him by a plexiglass screen.

"Orange isn't your color," I say.

"Shut up. How did you know to come?"

"Your roomie told me. What on earth has happened? Did you know Karim was busted too? Did you sell him pot?"

"Did I sell him pot!" Lynn laughs, but he looks angry. "Girl, you don't know shit! Where do you think I got all *my* stuff?"

"What are you talking about?"

"Karim is like a Balkan-Ozark kingpin. He's the strongest link in the local heroin supply chain. Well, he was."

"Wait a minute. You're telling me Karim was a dealer? I never saw any of that shit."

"You saw what you wanted to see, maybe."

Six Mile Store

"I swear to god, I thought he was an economics major. He never had any drugs! He can't even roll a joint!"

"Well, that's probably true. He told me a couple months back that he wasn't going to deal anymore, that he was going to go back to Turkey and close up shop. Hell, I thought he said you were going with him, pissed me off at the time. So I guess there weren't any drugs to see. Just a lot of money, the cops said."

"The police told you he had money? Why did they tell you that?"

Lynn was silent.

"Why did they tell you that shit, Lynn?"

"Because I told them what I know, OK? I told them everything I could. I'm trying to avoid going to prison here, all right?"

"So you destroyed Karim's life to save yourself? Real nice, Lynn."

"Come on, what was I supposed to do? My momma's in that hospice, you know she don't have anyone else to help her. We can't all be like you. We don't all just leave our families behind like something we scraped off our shoe."

I don't say a word. He softens. "Look, I'm not a hardened criminal who needs to be locked up forever. I just needed money to help Momma. I kept it low key, sold mostly to those college kids, just pot and uppers and so on. I never dealt the hardcore drugs. I sold a lot at that Baptist place you're at now. Plenty of profs asking for things, mostly Ritalin."

"I know that. But listen. How is Karim? Is he in there with you? Is he doing OK? I tried to ask when I came in, but they wouldn't tell me anything"

"Listen, now. This is important. And I hate to be the one to tell you. That cop you know, the one who's always in your face? He told me they've deported him."

Saturday, 5 December

When I get into work this afternoon, miserable and exhausted, all the girls are talking about how the Woodards have been busted too, for selling meth. Seems like the cops are coming down hard on everyone for drugs. But with the Woodards, all I can think about is what those little kids are going to eat once they get through all the bacon. Maybe they've got some decent relatives who will take them in, with mom and dad in jail.

"Hey Racecar," I say, as he walks through the door, the bell tinkling. Last time he was in, before his accident, he told me some stupid joke about a man with an orange for a head. I have another one ready for him, but I stop when I see his face.

The first thing that makes me realize something is different is the way he looks at us. Not with his usual easy cheerfulness, but more like we are under a microscope. He kind of glares at us, in fact. Then he doesn't say a word, just walks back to the cooler and gets a Mountain Dew. He brings it to the counter and I ask him for a dollar, which he gives me, then walks out.

"What was that?" I murmur to Michelle.

"He ain't been the same since that wreck. Rhonda said he ain't right. They couldn't afford for him to stay in the hospital so he got hisself discharged. But he doesn't know stuff."

Darren has forgotten us. The idea sticks right in my chest, like a piece of food I haven't been able to swallow correctly. He doesn't know me. But for years he's acted more like my dad than my real dad has. And now he doesn't know me? He doesn't remember my name, or the jokes we've told each other, or anything we have shared?

He looked through me, then walked away.

I'm not able to get much else done today. Sure, I go through the motions, but I find myself taking a long time to front the shelves, to stock the coolers. I don't want to see all of the faces I know. I want to forget them too.

The Cop comes in right at the wrong time. Michelle is out the back, bagging ice, and Lisa is hiding in the office as usual. I don't have much choice but to talk to him.

"Hey," I say, trying to look everywhere but his face.

"That Arab you've been seeing got sent away. He's gone for good," he says.

"I know. I saw Lynn yesterday."

"It was sorta funny, because he didn't actually have any drugs in the house. He had a lot of money, though, and some jewelry."

"He didn't wear jewelry."

"Yeah, well, we got on to him because around October time this little girl down at Fletcher Smith's gave us a call, said he came in and bought a big old diamond ring with

Six Mile Store

cash. She thought it wasn't likely that someone like him could do that. So she called us up. He put his real name on the paperwork. Looks like he was gonna take someone special somewhere real nice. Did I mention there were some first class plane tickets to Turkey in his dresser?"

I flush. The Cop notices.

"Sorry to break it to you. Turns out he had a married girlfriend. We caught up with her, asked her about the ring and the tickets. She fessed up. Told us she thought they were running away together. Told us he was dealing all kinds of things, and named everyone she knew who was working for him, too. After that we didn't really need the drugs. The money and the goods were enough. Those and your friend Lynn's statement, of course."

"Why are you here?"

"Just thought you'd want to know. You wanna know something else, too?

"No."

"Lynn mentioned that he had been supplying Ritalin to some of them professors at the Baptist college. More than they might need for personal use. Now, nobody around here is interested in seeing those gentlemen get in trouble. But I went to see Vowan. Kept it off the record for now. I tell you what, I don't like that guy."

"You and me both."

"I saw you upset last night, down at your boyfriend's house. You were upset when you got out of the car. Did he tell you about his other girlfriend?"

"No. I was there because I wanted to talk to him. I didn't know he was still seeing anyone else. And if you must know, I was upset because Vowan told me I couldn't keep my job. He said my teaching wasn't Christian enough, that the kids complained."

"Well, ain't that something," he said. "And with what he's been doing, too. Hmm. Seems to me with what I just told you, you could probably think of a way to keep your job."

"Why are you telling me all this? If everyone I know is dealing drugs, why don't you think I'm doing it too?"

"Girl, I've got my eye on you all the time. I know exactly what you do and don't do. I'm doing you a solid because I like you. Probably too much."

I take a deep breath, look directly in his eyes. "I don't like you."

He laughs. "Yes you do. You know exactly what you want, and you know I can give it to you." I don't reply. His smile fades. He leans over the counter, runs a finger lightly over my wrist. "And I promise, if you want me to, I will."

Sunday, 6 December

"I don't think she's great with the customers, you know. She can be an incredibly rude woman." Despite it all, being at work is soothing today: the mindlessness of the checkout, the familiar tinkle of the bell, the slowness of a Sunday morning. It's a rare pleasure, too, talking to Rhonda on days like this when she is a little like her old self, laughing like she used to, before she put that stillborn baby in the trash, before The Cop had to arrest her, before her trial and acquittal.

We look out the window at the yellow wintry sky. We see Billy Wayne starting over, coming to get his morning rolls of toilet paper, no doubt. What on earth *does* he do with all that toilet paper?

"What's Billy Wayne wearing this time? A red dickey? That's a new one," I say. Billy Wayne looks a little dazed. "Hey, Rhonda, whose car is that over at his house?"

"I don't know, but it was there last night too," she said. "Maybe they finally got some home help for his poor old momma. You know she hasn't let me in for months, even though we're kin? She won't even speak to me through the door these days."

I watch as Billy Wayne continues across the road, wearing his weird red bib. As he gets closer I can see something isn't right. There's no bib, or any shirt at all. The red is gushing blood. He reaches the edge of the parking lot, just off the road, then falls over right before the far pump, pumping out his own fuel right there onto the concrete.

Like with Michelle's finger, and like that day Racecar flipped, I am startled to find myself quietly taking charge. *Yes, 911, we have a man bleeding to death on our property. He lives across the street. His name is Billy Wayne Terrell. He looks after his elderly mother. There may be some home help in his house.* Sam Legs runs out with a couple of towels from the counter, holds them to Billy Wayne's neck, but I think he's already dead. It looks like his blood is leaking now, not pumping anymore.

Late that night, when everything is over—when it is finally quiet, and the last of the police have turned off back down Vilonia way, leaving me alone to close up after my unexpected double shift—I turn off the pumps and lock the door, then I walk out into the night. I pause next to my car.

There is one thing I have never tried. I get into my car and set the tripometer to zero. Then I pull carefully on to the deserted highway, heading west.

The lights of Conway seem to brighten as I approach, but I keep going. I keep going much farther than I think I need to. Six miles is longer than you imagine—that is, if you believe you're simply going to the city limits. I pass the

Six Mile Store

Waffle House. I pass the steakhouse. I pass the Chamber of Commerce and a First Baptist, a Second Baptist, a Ninth Baptist, a Nazarene. I keep going, in a line as straight as I can, and when the tripometer clicks over to 6 miles—right at Fletcher Smith's; I try not to look—a crossbuck shines out at me from the darkness. The railroad tracks.

I know, then. The faith healer had told me to look for a sign. This one says: go.

CONWAY POLICE DEPARTMENT
Voluntary Statement

Date of Statement: 13 October 1998
Time: 13:45   Place: Conway PD
Full legal name: Caroline Joanne Barnes
DOB: 5 September 1956
Address: 35 Cottonwood Ridge
City/Town: Saltillo   State: AR Zip: 72032

Statement given to: Lt. Wade Prescott

The above named officer has duly warned me that I have the following rights:

   That I have the right to remain silent and not make any statement at all; that any statement I make may be used as evidence against me in court; that I have the right to have a lawyer present to advise me prior to and during any questioning; that if I am unable to afford a lawyer, I have the right to have a lawyer appointed to advise me prior to and during any questioning; and that I have the right to terminate the interview at any time prior to and during the making of this statement.
   I have and do hereby knowingly, intelligently, and voluntarily waive the above explained rights and I do make the following statement voluntarily to the

aforementioned person(s) of my own free will and without any promises and/or offers of leniency or favors and without compulsion or persuasion by any person or persons whomsoever.

I got three apartments over at the Octagon complex on Elm Street. One of my renters, Lynn Duran, has been a friend for a while. One time last year I found out he was selling drugs, so I gave him a warning, and far as I know, he quit. He always pays his rent on time so I try to stay out of his business.

Back in May, Lynn introduced me to his friend Demir when I was doing a check on his place. Demir asked for my phone number, and we started talking and then carrying on. He seemed real sweet at first. But he was just stringing me along. Last month he told me he was seeing someone else, so I cut it off with him, totally ruined my birthday.

Yesterday, the law came to my house and said they thought Demir was dealing drugs and would I come here and make a statement. I don't do drugs and I got nothing to do with his drugs but I'll tell you my opinions.

If you're looking for Demir's connections, you might want to talk to Lynn Duran, my renter. If you ask me, he's probably selling marijuana, Ritalin, acid, and heroin. I also reckon you could talk to my old schoolmate Lisa Sellers. She told me she had some extra money coming in, and I thought that was odd, but now I wonder if she's dealing drugs too. It wouldn't surprise me none because she does all sorts of tacky ass shit.

Signed under the pains and penalties of perjury

CONWAY POLICE DEPARTMENT
Voluntary Statement

Date of Statement: 3 December 1998
Time: 13:45   Place: Conway PD
Full legal name: Caroline Joanne Barnes
DOB: 5 September 1956
Address: 35 Cottonwood Ridge
City/Town: Saltillo   State: AR Zip: 72032

Statement given to: Lt. Wade Prescott

The above named officer has duly warned me that I have the following rights:

That I have the right to remain silent and not make any statement at all; that any statement I make may be used as evidence against me in court; that I have the right to have a lawyer present to advise me prior to and during any questioning; that if I am unable to afford a lawyer, I have the right to have a lawyer appointed to advise me prior to and during any questioning; and that I have the right to terminate the interview at any time prior to and during the making of this statement.
I have and do hereby knowingly, intelligently, and voluntarily waive the above explained rights and I do make the following statement voluntarily to the

aforementioned person(s) of my own free will and without any promises and/or offers of leniency or favors and without compulsion or persuasion by any person or persons whomsoever.

  I don't even know why yall brought me in here again. I already made one statement about my ex-boyfriend Demir. I got nothing to do with his drugs or any jewelry or plane tickets they talked about. I aint seen him since July and I sure as hell wouldn't be going to Turkey with him if he is screwing someone else.

Signed under the pains and penalties of perjury

LISA

Friday, 17 July

I squinted suspiciously at Caroline. She was looking trimmer, yes, despite that blueberry muffin—and a little smug. "What's got you so happy," I asked, stirring Sweet'n Low into my coffee.

She smirked a little, brushing muffin crumbs from her tits. She wasn't wearing a bra, which in my opinion made her look a little sloppy. "Lisa, I could just as well ask you why you don't cheer the fuck up. You know I mentioned my tall, dark, and handsome friend? Demir?"

Caroline had been seeing some kid behind her husband's back. I knew it; she had never said it out loud, but I could tell. She talked about her "friend," but what middle-aged woman is friends with a 20-year-old boy? It only made sense if they were going to bed together.

"Anyway, he gave me this rich perfume," she continued, holding her wrist out to me. It smelled like band-aids, but I wasn't about to say that to her. "And he says he's got a lot more money waiting to come in. I think I might be in love. I'm ready to skip this country. Who needs sleet in winter?" She let out an irritating chuckle of laughter.

Shit, girl, you don't even have a passport, I thought. "What kind of money?"

Caroline leaned closer. "OK, I'll tell you. Remember my tenant Lynn, who lives in that apartment out by the train tracks? Well, he's a dealer. He works for Demir. He's actually how we met. Lynn hooked me up with him when I was looking for a little pick me up."

I wasn't shocked; I knew a prof up at the Baptist college from my aerobics class. She was outwardly the best sort of church lady, but I knew she took Ritalin to get through those boring lectures.

"Anyway, Demir has some of the really good stuff, the stuff that sells for decent money, but Lynn is no good at getting rid of it. Lynn says his customers only want pot and uppers, acid sometimes. Nobody wants...heroin," she whispered.

Now this was a surprise to me. Out my way, everyone wanted to be out of their minds on drugs all the time. It seemed to me heroin would be the best thing to sell, if you had it. "Why don't they want it?" I asked.

"Well, he sells to those college kids. They don't want it; maybe they're too busy pretending they have a future," she said, again with that trashy little giggle.

"So you're saying he needs someone to help him sell it," I said. I considered it. I had a bunch of fucked-up neighbors I bet could use a fix, but I wasn't about to get involved with people who knew where I lived. But it occurred to me that Rhonda might be able to help me out. Down there at that store she owns, she said they had all kinds of characters coming in day and night. And if I could get a good cut, that would be the end of my worries about Charlotte's dance outfits—I could get those and more. Maybe I could even get a new car. The one I got now is a rat trap, dents everywhere, key permanently stuck in the ignition, one window stuck a crack open so it's cold all winter and hot all summer. I'm surprised it even runs. "Why don't you let me find out—I think I know someone."

Sunday, 19 July

After I visited the store and left Rhonda my number, she called later on yesterday evening. She sounded dead tired. I said I would be more than happy to help her out. I even made up some story about how the girls behind the counter had acted unprofessional to me when I walked in. I told her that she needed an adult in there and I would definitely do a better job keeping an eye on things, if Rhonda needed the help for a while. Naw, sugar, we can talk about paychecks later, I said. I don't need much; you know my husband does really well.

She hired me.

Today I had to get trained by that girl with that thing on her leg. Sam. I endured the slow business of selling cigarettes and gas, waiting for the Sunday morning bikers I knew were coming in. When they swaggered into the place, I cornered one guy with a marijuana leaf patch on his jacket. I asked him, quietly by the diapers, "Hey, I've got some stuff coming. Do your guys ever need some...stuff? Maybe even more than you can use yourself?" He grinned—these bikers are always such polite guys.

"Yes ma'am, I believe we could," he said. And that was that.

I spent my afternoon getting bored shitless by that other little girl, who kept telling me about her own Turkish boyfriend. How many of them can there be? Clinton evidently ain't worth a shit, if we've got Mexicans and Arabs running all over Conway, Arkansas.

After my shift, I went home smelling like gas and onions. Thank god I don't have to keep this up for long. I called Caroline and told her to put me in touch with Demir.

Monday, 20 July

I tell you what, I have never been more uncomfortable than last night meeting Demir in that park over at Toad Suck. It was a good place to go, since nobody I know lives over in that part of town. I thought he'd give me the drugs when I got there, but for some reason he said he had to go get it from a friend. Why the hell didn't he bring it with him? He asked me if I wanted to come to his house to get it! Hell no, I thought, but I tried to be polite when I declined.

We agreed a drop-off at the store, which felt a little safer to me since I planned to sell it out of the office there anyway. I said I could wrap up the money and drop it in the toilet cistern; he would come in and make a swap: my cash for his drugs.

The first thing I learned is that I wasn't going to make any extra money—not for now, anyway. I was going to have to sell marijuana now, and I had to pay the full retail price because Demir couldn't "trust" me yet. I have to prove myself. If it goes good, then he'll give me more soon. That's OK. I can do it.

Six Mile Store

The next thing I learned was when Demir came round to make a drop. Turns out he's a. k. a. Karim—the one who's supposed to be studying economics down at one of them colleges. Studying economics! Not the way she's thinking! And I guess she don't have the first clue that she ain't his only girlfriend neither. What a little dumb shit.

Still, it will make the drop-offs a little easier, Demir or Karim or whatever his name is, if he at least has a reason to be here—if he can get over to the Six Mile without getting pulled over, that is. Everybody knows these cops are prejudiced as shit.

Tuesday, 21 July

I'm worn out and sore from working in the store today. That little cock-legged bitch made me bag up about 300 pounds of ice before I left. At least I got some of the marijuana bagged up and stashed away behind that cheap dog food nobody ever buys. I wonder if that shit is even still good. Nobody ever seems to look at the dates on the cans.

The worst part was that hillbilly Woodard telling those girls I was his cousin. As if I'd be related to that trash. When I went out there he informed me that I was working on his turf! I didn't know there were property lines, I told him, and he laughed at me. "We sell the meth here. If you're selling it too, we're going to have to come to an agreement."

"I ain't selling meth, mister," I said. "I don't know what you think or why you think it, but you'd better think again."

I wouldn't have to demean myself this way if my husband could take care of us like he promised when I married him. He told me I'd never have to work. It was so nasty what he said last week at dinner—well, yelled, really, with his face that ugly red it sometimes gets if he's mad, or if he's

Six Mile Store

been drinking. Get a job? What about Lottie? I looked at her there, eating her little nuggets. Plenty of nuggets for plenty of protein for plenty of muscles. I know she's going to be an amazing dancer. "Can I go to my room and play with my Game Boy?" she asked.

"You go on ahead, baby," I said. "I'm just here talking to daddy."

"Yelling at daddy, more like," she sighed, shoving her chair back and stalking out of the room. That was totally unfair. *I* haven't been yelling at all.

It was like he hadn't heard a dern thing. "I want you to get out there tomorrow and find something to do. I ain't paying for you to sit around and decorate the mantelpiece or whatever the shit..." He trailed off as he looked around at the new Snow Babies on the windowsill. This year they came out with some real cuties.

"I have a job, Duane," I said. "I have Charlotte. She needs me to be home for her recitals and to make her costumes and to make her lunches and to get her hair done and..."

"That's the other thing," he said. "No. More. Recitals. The kid can't dance for shit, Lisa. It's money down the drain."

I stood up and in one motion swiped his plate of spaghetti onto the floor, where it slammed down with a big old smash. I wished I could smash his face into it, watch his stupid red cheeks blend in with the sauce. We looked at each other, both shocked at what I had done. I knew then I had put myself in a risky situation. "Don't tell me what to do," I whispered, and then I walked out, before he could retaliate.

Just because I want a nice car and a pretty house and I want to keep our daughter occupied, he thinks I'm wasting money. That is some bullshit. All he's done is show me that I can't trust him to be the man he said he was.

Sitting on my bed I could hear him blasting the TV, some dumbass football game. I tried to gear myself up to go back into the kitchen and clean up all the broken spaghetti mess. I wondered why I can't be more like Caroline, with a husband like hers who is out of town most of the time, and plenty of money, and time for all kinds of extracurriculars...

Well, I guess now I've done what he told me to do, now that I'm working down at the Six Mile. But he ain't gonna see a cent of this money I'm about to make on the drugs. I'm gonna use it to divorce his ass and take everything I can from him and get Lottie onto the pageant circuit. Maybe even get her into movies. See how he likes that.

Saturday, 5 September

I was so glad to have a day off from that place. I hate the way my hands smell like onions after I've been making sandwiches for Mexicans all day. That pissant little store is not what I saw for myself when I was homecoming queen, that's for damn sure. I might get a paycheck at the end of the week for a grand total of $125.00. But when I finally get the heroin, I should be riding high.

That cop came in yesterday, the handsome one who hangs out here sometimes. He told us more kids got caught with pot in their lockers down at Vilonia when the school year started up again. I kinda felt a little uncomfortable—I sold the last of Demir's most recent pot drop to those bikers last Sunday, and who knows what they do with it. So I said he ought to go up and talk to them Woodards up Palarm way if he's worried about drugs. I've been seeing that truck drive up and down in front of my house a little more often than I'd like over the last couple months. I guess Mr. Woodard is gonna learn what it feels like to be intimidated. That'll teach him to mess with me.

A. M. Belsey

I talked to Caroline on the phone tonight, just to say happy birthday. She was all upset because Demir told her last night he didn't want to see her anymore, just didn't feel that way about her. I ain't heard her this pissed off since her husband had that affair down in Gulf Shores. She swore blind she was gonna get even with Demir somehow, maybe even tell the cops about him.

I stopped her and said not to say anymore, just to have a drink and cool off. I reminded her that if Demir gets in trouble, I probably will too. She seemed to calm down. I didn't want to get her mad again, so I didn't tell her about that little girl at the store. I don't reckon she needs to know any of that right now. I'll keep it for another time.

It feels good to be the one in charge of the secrets for once.

Sunday, 13 September

Demir finally dropped off some more pot last Thursday. He left me one of them blue notes saying the next delivery will be the "big one" but there won't be any more after that. He says I have to sell it as soon as possible. I wished he'd stop putting my name on them notes; it's like he wants me to get caught. I burned it in the trash pile when I got home.

When the bikers came in this morning, I said they should come back for the good stuff in a couple of weeks. I told Mr Marijuana Leaf that my supply chain was blocked. I thought that sounded good. He snorted at me and took the pot. I've got smart over the past few weeks, upped the price a little, cut in a little oregano to make it all go further, but not enough that anyone could tell. Every little helps. I put all my profits in my divorce fund.

I usually try not to think too hard about whatever has gone wrong that I've only ever gone from Springfield to Saltillo in my life. When I was in high school, I had it all: decent grades, a good-looking boyfriend, popularity, parties every weekend, a ticket to a bright future. But I didn't really like college, and I dropped out after a couple of years. I started working little temp jobs here and there, staying with Momma and Daddy until they got sick of it and told me to find my own place. I moved in with Caroline for a while, watched her bring every Jethro and his brother home until she found one she liked enough to keep for a while, though god knows she didn't pick a winner, when it came down to it.

But I guess I can't talk. I met Duane down at the honky-tonk, and he talked a big game about how he was gonna make a lot of money, build a big house by the lake, spend every weekend on jet skis, and vacations down the Gulf every summer. And I fell for it all, like the dumbass I am.

11 years later, I'm stuck and I'm old. But I tell you what, six months from now I'll still be old, but I won't be stuck anymore. That's for damn sure.

Saturday, 17 October

I sat there on one of them hard-ass little benches they put out for parents to wait on, trying to squirm my skirt back down to my knees. The other moms come in all dolled up like they've been out for lunch somewhere, so I thought today I'd make a special effort, since I ain't been in for a few weeks. I couldn't resist spending a little of my Six Mile money on a cute little off-the-shoulder number which I put on with some fall boots. I guess I was thinking about what I used to wear when I met Duane—maybe a little sexy for the afternoon, but I liked it. Maybe I'd go out in the evening, see if Caroline wants to do some line dancing.

Duane's been taking Lottie in to Miss Jennifer's dance classes on the days I've been working, but he don't say much about it afterwards. So when I take her in, I stay to watch, unlike him. Some of them scrawny little girls look so serious, their eyes staring out to nowhere, hands straight up, noses in the air. But Lottie puts a little shimmy in her moves, makes up her own drama. She ain't a follower.

When the class ended, Miss Jennifer came over and said, "Mrs. Sellers, could we have a chat about Lottie?" My stomach turned over. I could see Claire's mom, Denise something or other, craning her neck to listen in. She had her head turned like a bird. *Eat a worm, Denise,* I thought. *You could use the calories.*

"Mrs. Sellers, glad to see you. I've been trying to catch your husband, but he's real busy. I'm glad you came in today." I smiled at her, didn't say nothing yet. I wished we were alone. Out of the corner of my eye, I saw another mom, Trish, walking up to where Denise was standing. I could feel them staring holes into us. But Jennifer said, "Do you know about Ballet Arkansas?"

My heart skipped. I do know about Ballet Arkansas. I remember Chelsea Clinton used to dance with them before she swanned off to D.C.

Jennifer went on. "Well, they do casting in the community for their special productions, you know, The Nutcracker and so on. Now, it's too late for this year, but I'd really like to get Lottie to...focus. I think with some dedicated practice and maybe your help with some other changes, she could be ready to try out next August."

Nearly a year from now? "You don't think she could do it this Christmas?" I asked. I could see it now, Lottie as Clara, doing the prettiest little *pas de deux.*

I heard Denise let out a snotty little giggle. I tried to ignore her jealousy. Everyone can see her Claire's the ugliest little girl in class. With those ears flapping out, she's probably got too much wind resistance to do more than one twirl at a time.

"Well, like I said, they've already done their casting for this year's performances. And Lottie really needs to focus on getting her basic moves polished. Plus, if she wants to perform at Robinson Center, she's got to slim down. I just want to set her a goal. I think in a few months, with a better diet and a little more exercise, she could definitely be ready. To audition, I mean."

Denise was whispering now. I heard her say something that sounded like "fat ass." I looked over at Lottie, who was sitting with her feet straight out in front of her, hunched over her Game Boy. She must have shoved it in her ballet bag when I wasn't looking. Her legs looked strong to me, not like Trish's kid Jessica. *Her* bony legs made her look like a malnourished baby deer. But she did get the lead in that last recital. I looked straight at the other two moms. They pretended not to be listening. *Let them choke on it when Lottie is famous*, I thought. *Eat a worm. Go wild. Eat two.*

"Thank you, Miss Jennifer. I would love for Lottie to audition for Ballet Arkansas," I said, voice carrying across the room.

Lottie glanced up at the sound of her name. "Gimme a second to finish this level," she said. The other little girls were heading out the door with their mothers. I could have sworn I heard Trish say "dressed like a crack whore" as she left with Denise, both sniggering.

Well. Not crack, Trish. Heroin. And I remember you from school, if you want to talk about whores.

When I got home, Duane was sitting on his ass on the couch, beer in hand, golf on the television. Lottie ambled into the kitchen, her eyes still on Tetris. "There's string cheese in the fridge, baby," I called. I parked myself on the other side of the couch. "Guess what. Miss Jennifer says

Lottie has huge potential. Huge. She's recommending her to audition for Ballet Arkansas."

Duane took a swig of his beer. I noticed two other cans crunched up on the floor next to him. "That so?" he said, eyes not moving from the television.

"That's right, Duane. She says that with some work, Lottie can be really something." Lottie came back through, smiling. I hope she heard me.

"Hey Daddy," she said, then headed up the hall to her room. I heard her door click shut.

"Of course she did, Lisa. She wants more of my money."

"My money, you mean. I'm paying for it now. Remember? You made me get a job."

Duane belched. "Gas station minimum wage ain't gonna cut it, sweetheart. You think I can't do math? You can barely put gas in your own car."

I laughed. I liked that Duane didn't know. I imagined him walking into an empty house one day soon: no snacks, no kid, no wife to knock around. But Duane didn't like that laugh, not one bit. His eyes swiveled to me, red raw. I knew I was in trouble, but I couldn't stop myself. "She's going places. Not like you. And I'm going with her."

Despite the beer, Duane was still faster than I gave him credit for. In a moment, he was over me, one hand on my throat. "Let's get one thing straight, Lisa. You ain't going nowhere." His breath was sour, gasping into my face as he pinched my upper arm, hard, his body pushing mine into the cushions. "What in the hell are you wearing? Do you think you can still get away with this shit?" He tore at my new dress, ripping the sleeve down, exposing my breast.

Six Mile Store

"Get off me," I whispered, trying to get my knee up like I knew I should, trying to get an elbow into his neck or something. I didn't want to scream. Lottie's door was closed, but she might run out if she heard commotion. I didn't want her to see me degraded like this. Duane leaned on me harder. I felt him fumbling with his belt, heard the buckle clatter against the coffee table. I felt his stubble scraping at my face. I squeezed my eyes together and went limp.

It was mean, like always. He took a handful of my hair and kept my head pulled down—I guess he learned his lesson after that bloody nose from last time. And he made sure both of my wrists were caught one way or another. But I wasn't fighting. I took myself to another place. I pictured someone handsome, a good-looking tall man, wearing a police uniform. I imagined him driving up to the house, looking through the window, watching. Duane moved one of his hands to my hip, digging his fingers in violently, possessively. I thought about the money I would make, the apartment I would move into, the blue-eyed police officer coming to check on me, staying over for dinner.

Duane collapsed onto me, heavy. I shoved him away, tried to pull my ruined dress back together. Lottie's door—still closed. "You ain't going nowhere," Duane repeated. I didn't say a damn word, just got up and went to my bedroom. I tried to call Caroline, see if she wanted to head out to Electric Cowboy later. But I just got her machine.

Sunday, 1 November

I didn't tell Demir I've never cut up heroin before, but with my brains I was able to figure out how many little bags I should end up with. I've got 60 bags here. It was supposed to be 50, but God helps those who help themselves, and I've got the ingenuity, and the baby powder.

When Mr Marijuana Leaf finally came in today, I followed him to the back of the store and we stood out by the ice bagging area, where nobody could hear us. "I've got the good stuff," I said, and showed him a baggie. "60 bags. What do you want to take it in?" I was proud of myself for the way I said that. Always be closing the deal, they say.

But he laughed at me. "60 bags of meth that look like that? Why you trying to sell us powder? Old Woodard always sells us the crystal. It's better."

I stared at him. "This isn't meth. It's heroin. Heroin!"

"What?" he said, then laughed out loud, really loud. I glanced up at the counter, but the girls weren't paying any attention. "I don't want heroin, and if I did, I wouldn't

Six Mile Store

want 60 bags of it, you freak," he hissed, which was extremely rude in my opinion.

"Well if you did want heroin, how many bags *would* you want?" I asked. My mother didn't raise a shy girl. I can give as good as I get.

"Fuuuuck. Give me twenty. I can probably find someone who still does this shit."

Twenty! But what was I going to do with the rest?

After he gave me the money for the 20 bags, he went out to meet his friends in the parking lot. As I looked out the window, they all glanced back. I could see them laughing. I wasn't laughing, though. I was down a few hundred bucks and stuck with 40 bags of heroin.

Sunday, 29 November

That good-looking cop came in here again, telling me my info was good before. He said they've been investigating those Woodards and found out they'd been dealing meth all over Mayflower. He said I should look out for some news. He seemed impressed that I had known anything in the first place, and he asked me if I knew anything else. I said I'd keep my eyes open.

I guess I wasn't on his radar. But if these podunk-ass cops were finally doing their damn jobs and cracking down on drugs, I knew Demir was right: I *had* to get rid of that heroin fast. Now, I knew there was no more evidence on me in particular: the drugs were in the safe, and I dumped the wrappers and burned all them blue papers Demir kept writing my name on as receipts. But I'd be a fool if I thought Demir wouldn't tell that cop exactly who sold that shit for him.

I called Caroline, hoping to get some advice, but she was real offish with me on the phone, said she didn't have time to talk.

Six Mile Store

I finally had a brainwave. I know it's not just bikers who take drugs. I read that book *Christiane F* a while ago. I know those working girls are addicts. They'd probably buy everything I've got. Then I could get out of this stupid game before I get busted, figure out something else for money, just go ahead and divorce Duane and take everything I can get. But as far as I knew there weren't any prostitutes coming into the store.

Thank goodness for weird old Billy Wayne. When I remembered what the kids said about him getting in trouble with his momma for calling hookers, I had an idea. I caught him this morning about ten, when he came in for his toothpicks. I followed him outside and said, "Hey Billy Wayne, I hear you like to talk to pretty ladies on the phone. Is that right?"

His face flashed kind of pale, then he said, "Well, it's nice to talk to girls."

I said, "Billy Wayne, do any of the girls you talk to live close? Do you ever think about asking one of them to come over and see you?"

"My momma's at home. I ain't bringing girls into momma's home. She said I ain't allowed that."

"Well, Billy Wayne, I've got something I'd like to give to one of those ladies you talk to sometimes. Do you want to help me? You could always wait until your momma is asleep, couldn't you? You can talk to her or whatever and then just call me when she's ready to go. Hell, you could even have a sleepover. I could come by and chat with her first thing the next morning."

Billy Wayne was silent for a long time, looking out over the field next to the store, the one where that lonesome run-down old Fischer place is sitting. Finally, he said, "I reckon maybe I could. Next weekend."

Sunday, 6 December

That Woodard bust everyone was talking about yesterday had me spooked. But Billy Wayne said he would call a lady this weekend, and sure enough, he did. A car rolled up his driveway last night about 9pm—and it was funny, I don't ever remember seeing a car over there apart from Billy Wayne's old clapped out blue Ford LTD. The car was still there at 10:30 when I closed up the store, so I reckoned he was having a good time. Having that sleepover we talked about.

I parked in the rear lot and slipped into the back door of the Six Mile first thing this morning to get the baggies out of the safe, ready to take them over the road to meet whatever girl Billy Wayne had been hanging out with all night. As I was about to leave, I heard Rhonda's horrible sick cackle of a laugh, its grating screech. What on earth was she doing at the store?

I swept the baggies into my purse and left as quietly as I had come in. I trudged in the weeds behind the abandoned Fischer house, which was out of the line of sight of the registers, then over the road and back around Rhonda's house, and finally into Billy Wayne's back yard. I knocked on his kitchen door. "Billy Wayne, let me in so I can talk to the lady," I said, and pulled down the handle on the screen. It wasn't locked.

I opened the screen door up and stepped into the filthiest kitchen I had ever seen. I put my purse on the table, opened it up, ready to get my business finally done, get the hell out of there.

"Billy Wayne, I need to ask your lady friend if she wants any of this..." I began, then stopped as I walked into the living room. There was a peculiar odor in the house, like drains or rats, and the whole place was a disgusting mess. "Billy Wayne, does your momma ever help you do the clea—" I started, but stopped as I saw Billy Wayne, knelt on his bedroom floor with a roll of toilet paper. He was wrapping it around something that looked an awful lot like an arm. I realized a moment later that it *was* an arm, with long fingernails poking out the bottom, where he hadn't yet done the final wrapping.

I looked behind him, and on the bed there was what looked like a big stuffed animal, or an overwrapped mummy.

The mummy was shaped like a woman, and it even wore a big dress, a flowered muumuu-type affair. "Billy Wayne," I whispered, "where's your momma?"

Billy Wayne looked up at me, surprised. Maybe he didn't hear me coming in, engrossed in his grotesque project. "Don't you look at my momma!" he yelled, dropping the stiff little arm with its pathetic pink fingernails. I muffled a scream with my sleeve and ran back through the house to the back door, but he caught me just as I made it into the

Six Mile Store

kitchen. He shoved me against the counter, banging my hip into the counter's edge.

I forced him away, knee into his groin while poking my fingers into his face, and I grabbed a dirty kitchen knife from the sink. I sunk it into his neck while he was cowering and covering his eyes, which I guess I'd hurt. I hoped I did. I pulled the knife out and put it back in again. Then I ran: back around Rhonda's house, back across the road, back behind the old Fischer house. Maybe people saw me running on the road, maybe they didn't. It's quiet on a Sunday morning, when everyone is in church. I got around to my car at the back of the store, then drove it up toward Saltillo, so nobody would see me pulling out on to the road, and then just kept on driving. Maybe nobody would ever know I had been there at all.

Well shit. What I am going to do? After I got past Saltillo I started going any which way, until I realized I was in a place I was familiar with. Far too familiar. Somehow I had got myself turned around and ended up in Springfield, which isn't so much as a place as a pit in the ground—and, by the way, it's the pit where I was brung up. It looks like I can't get away from this hellhole even if I try.

I pulled my car off the road at Cadron Creek and decided to walk out to the old bridge. Why they keep that shit around littering up the place I don't know. They say it's supposed to be a historic treasure or whatever, but all it ever was as far as I was concerned was an ugly place to get your legs broken or drown yourself.

It's cold out here, with the dirty slush that never fully melts in these woods once it snows. The air even *smells* cold, too, like woodsmoke and stagnant water. I clomp down to the water and sit on a soggy log. The woods are silent. I guess anything that wants to be alive hasn't stayed here.

I don't have a coat on. I see now that I have blood on my shirt, which isn't a surprise when it comes down to it. I go to reach in my purse for a cigarette—not that I smoke anymore, I keep them there just in case—and it turns out I'm not carrying my purse.

And I know I didn't leave it in the car—because now I know I left it at Billy Wayne's house.

Maybe it's OK. Maybe I can say Billy Wayne stole my purse. Maybe I won't have to watch Lottie grow up from behind a plexiglass screen. Maybe I don't need to go out here and hang myself from the Springfield-Des Arc Bridge. Maybe I—

THE ENDING

The ambulance came, and the police, and there was a big to-do on Highway 64, with them trying to route people to the back of the store, getting them to drive up around the old Fischer place to bypass the blood evidence on the highway. All that meadow got torn up with tire tracks and mud.

By that afternoon, everywhere from Enola to Vilonia was buzzing with gossip about what had happened at Billy Wayne's house. All of our regulars descended on the store, desperate to talk shit about him, how they had always suspected he was a pervert. Of course, they never had. Most of us thought he was harmless. Weird, but not threatening.

But then JC Bristow, the farmer in the house up the lane behind Rhonda, came in and said Billy Wayne's momma had told him and his wife Wanda years ago that Wanda needed to be careful in the garden. Billy Wayne's momma said he probably wasn't too safe, that he had got in trouble with the police for looking up local call girls in the phone book and scaring them over the phone. And then the next thing they heard from her, Billy Wayne had bit a chunk out of one of the home help nurses the hospital had sent around. The woman didn't press charges, just up and left the state, JC said, and after that Wanda stopped doing farm work outside.

Even with that, though, at first I didn't believe the stories people were telling, that Billy Wayne had his dead mother in the house, all wrapped up and looking like a mangled porcupine with layers of toilet paper and toothpicks he used to hold her together.

But it got worse real quick: everyone all of a sudden started saying that old Billy Wayne had murdered Patrice Watson, a girl *everyone* knew from school, the sort of girl who knew everyone in town.

Then The Cop told us Lisa's purse had been found in Billy Wayne's house, and it had a bunch of heroin in it. He said they had been keeping their eyes on her. But with Billy Wayne having done what he did, right now they were more worried about her wellbeing, and had we seen her? But we hadn't. And why would her purse be at Billy Wayne's? And how could Lisa be involved, anyway? It had to be a misunderstanding, surely.

But in practical terms, without Lisa the store was short staffed for the evening, and with all the extra foot traffic we were getting it would have been crazy to close up. I offered to cover the night shift too, and to get the cash envelopes ready for Monday's bank run. The office was a real mess. Lisa had left shit everywhere, as always, but something under the desk caught my eye. It was a piece of blue scented paper with a note on it: *Lisa: this is the last one. Like I said, get it done fast. -Demir*

Six Mile Store

I didn't know who Demir was, but I knew Karim's handwriting—and his stationery—when I saw it.

I could see the truth now, or some of it. Lisa had been dealing for Karim too. But how? I wondered where that lying two-faced bitch had disappeared to. And now I had nothing—no relationship, no MA, no plan, no future—and nobody to talk to about any of it. I shoved Karim's note into my pocket and came out of the office, numb, and served out the rest of my double shift—the last shift I would ever do at the Six Mile Store.

When I found myself at the train tracks that night, I thought the faith healer had sent me a sign that I should just get out. Go to another country, meet people who aren't like me, build a new life, forget any of this shit ever happened.

I thought about it real hard. But you know what won out in the end? I didn't want that asshole Vowan to win. Even if I had to stick around a little longer, I wanted to be the one to jerk a knot in his tail. And maybe, deep down, a part of me knows I can never get out of this hellhole, even if I try.

So instead I went to my dorm and beat on the door until the RA let me in. She raged at me about how I was late. I walked right past her and went to bed. And first thing on Monday I went to Vowan's office and said I knew what he was doing, and I wasn't prepared to leave unless I took him down with me. I liked watching his ugly face turn yellow when I told him that I had heard it all from The Cop.

That was a huge risk, but it paid off. I've been here for two years now, finishing up my degree, working alongside Vowan every day. He knows better than to say a single goddamn word to me. I got to see Kim graduate; she moved out to Seattle. I've become as much a part of this little Baptist college now as I ever was that store on those ill-fated crossroads. I imagine I'll be here until something better comes along, or until The Cop tells me to stop working so I can be at home for him full time.

Every Friday, The Cop picks me up from my dorm, takes me to his spacious, cool, sanitized house, holds me down on his spacious, cool, sanitized bed. I stare at the diamond dust popcorn ceiling. I'm fascinated by how his eyes glimmer under his eyebrows, like jewels in a smuggler's cave. He commands me. I'll never resist him again.

But sometimes, in the moments before sleep, I can still hear music: exotic and mournful, lively and sweet. I can feel my heart soaring with almost-remembered melodies, and falling with them too. I recall how sometimes I couldn't stop myself from dancing, and sometimes the rhythm would drag me to Karim's room—neither of us could help it; we were pulled by the harmonies, pushed into each other, choreographed by insane Bulgarians on keyboard and oboe and clarinet. They charmed us like snakes in the hot humid night.

The songs were the soundtrack to my lonely life, on the few nights I could pretend not to be lonely anymore.

I've obliterated them from my waking mind.

TOMORROW

The store will always be there. It's modern and gleaming now, a beacon of light for travellers moving from nowhere to nowhere. Push the door open. The bell tinkles. The polished tiles grin. The air smells of pre-packaged snacks, beef jerky, and pizzas warmed under bright lights. The young women behind the counter greet you.

You live six miles away from it. You pass it all the time, usually at high speed, trying not to make eye contact with it. It's always been entwined with death, but now it sings to you like a siren: songs about people who have forgotten you, and those you're desperate to forget. Each drive by is a struggle between the urge to look and the need to move. Are you moving forward?

The store is still there, and it will always be there, and you can't avoid it. It sits at a crossroads, daring you to turn.

Acknowledgements

I do not recommend taking over twenty years to write anything, let alone a novella, but we are where we are. Over many years and many iterations of this story, several people have either offered to read or been pressed into it out of a sense of obligation. I deeply appreciate every person who has been involved in making Six Mile Store better than it would have been had I tried to do it alone.

Thank you especially to my long-suffering editor, Delphine Gatehouse, who on one hand wanted me to make this story longer, but on the other probably didn't want to look at it for a further twenty years. And thank you to my husband, Giles, who has always given me the space and time to do anything that makes me happy.

Thank you, thank you, thank you to my readers: Libby Alderman, Bibi Berki, Noah Brand, Josh Crome, Anne Currie, Lynn Duran (he doesn't really sell drugs), Jason Fischer, Jessica Gregson, Ben Henley, Rohini Janakarajah, Genevieve Jenner, Alex Jones (not that one), Rich Jones, Chris King, Susan Johnson Mumford, John McGraw, Jessica Pavlos, Amy Qualls, Brooke Shelby-Stone, Kim Mize Terrell,

Beau Wilcox, and Thom Willis. There may be others I have forgotten. I hope not. But twenty years is a very long time. Please forgive me if I have left you out.

I finished this book at an artists' retreat, *Fai da Te!*, that changed my life. Thank you to Carmen Aleman, Cash Aspeek, Maria Teresa Gavazzi, Christina Lorimer, Julia Maddison, Emma Roper-Evans, Veronica Shimanovskaya, Chris Simpson, and Natalia Zagorksa-Thomas for allowing me to share a little bit of Heaven with them.

Last, and definitely least, thank you to the real Lisa. Without you I never would have had a villain.

www.ingramcontent.com/pod-product-compliance
Lightning Source LLC
LaVergne TN
LVHW040104080526
838202LV00045B/3774